Praise for Anne Goodwin's fiction

absorbing, clever and heartening
Alison Moore, author of Booker-shortlisted *The Lighthouse*

Anne Goodwin's prose is at once sensitive, invigorating and inspired Rebecca Root, actor

exudes authenticity The Psychologist

a pleasure to read from start to finish
North East Lifestyle magazine

tantalisingly grips the reader The Contemporary Small Press

complex, fascinating and highly contemporary Shiny New Books

will stay with you long after you've finished reading
Sanjida Kay, author of *Bone by Bone*

compelling, insightful and brave
Ashley Stokes, author of *The Syllabus of Errors*

every turn of a page is a revelation, an insight to human emotions
Judith Barrow, author of *The Memory*

genuine, believable, authentic and totally addictive
Fiction Books

a poignant story told with both sensitivity and humour
Left on the Shelf

a book of kindness, positivity and hope Emma B Books

one hell of a compelling read Ginger Book Geek

would definitely recommend this Twilight Reader

chilled me to the bone Colleen's Book Reviews

a tender and warm-hearted read GraceJReviewerlady

a truly immersive story that really gets under your skin
The Book Magnet

Goodwin's description and writing is superb Honestmamreader

*heartbreaking, funny and surprising all rolled into one good cup
of tea* The Book Review Crew

endearing and life affirming Reflections of a reader

Stolen Summers

A heartbreaking tale of betrayal, confinement and dreams of escape

Anne Goodwin

Annecdotal Press

Copyright © 2022 Anne Goodwin

Content warnings: incarceration, institutional abuse, racism, misogyny, forced adoption, self-harm, indirect reference to rape, bereavement.

First paperback edition

Editor: Sara-Jayne Slack

Proofreading: Michelle Watson & Clare Stevens

Cover design: 100Covers

ISBN (paperback) 978-1-7391450-0-2

ISBN (ebook) 978-1-7391450-1-9

Annecdotal Press

annegoodwin.weebly.com

For the women wounded by warped twentieth-century morality

Chapter 1: March, 1939

Not all the nuns were cruel. Some of the younger ones would address the girls kindly if Mother Superior were out of earshot. So Matilda counted her blessings when Sister Bernadette slipped onto the seat beside her in the taxicab, while a sombre man with a box-shaped head took the passenger seat at the front. He resembled a tradesman in his white cotton coat worn over an ordinary jacket and trousers; Matilda assumed the nuns had offered him a lift out of charity. He wasn't introduced.

Although still sore down below, she held herself erect with her hands folded in her lap. She had dressed for hopefulness that morning in the polka-dot frock her brother favoured; her wool coat with the missing button lay with her suitcase in the boot. Guided by the mirror of her compact, she had dusted her cheeks with rouge. Her hair was a fright but, once the salon had worked its magic, it would be as if the horrors of the past few months were another girl's history.

No one spoke on the journey; the sole sounds the purr of the engine and the intermittent striking of matches for the men's cigarettes. Matilda had almost nodded off when she opened her eyes to find they were on the road that passed Stainburn School.

Her bodice tugged against her bosom as she leant forward, then sideways, then back, searching in vain for a peep of mustard and maroon. She had thought she had seen enough changes for one lifetime when she first donned that uniform. She could not have imagined the turmoil to come.

The driver seemed unfamiliar with the area: instead of veering left towards Briarwood, he continued downhill towards the centre of town. As the tradesman turned his boxy head to speak to the cabbie, Matilda surmised he wanted dropping off at the shops. She tried to be tolerant, but she resented the delay. Her brother would be waiting, and minutes felt like hours to a six-year-old child.

The diversion afforded some consolation: a chance to reacquaint herself with the town where she was born. She had left it for an overnight stay on three occasions in her almost twenty years. If she fulfilled her ambition to train as a nanny, she would have to leave again, and for longer. But not until Henry was old enough for boarding school.

Nearer the town centre, daffodils bowed to the headstones in St Mark's churchyard. Weeds would have colonised her mother's grave in her absence; Matilda resolved to take Henry to tidy the plot tomorrow if the weather held.

They skirted the brewery. Even with the windows closed Matilda smelled the hops. She could not ask, but wondered if Sister Bernadette secretly relished this exposure to masculine vices. Neither alcohol nor nicotine crossed the threshold of the convent.

As the cab proceeded out of town, something nagged at Matilda's mind like an aching tooth on biting into a toffee apple.

Shuffling her hands in her lap, she pushed her apprehension away. Sister Bernadette fingered her rosary. The tradesman lit another cigarette. Surely the driver could have taken him to the bus station if he had business elsewhere?

Matilda's irritation vanished as she glimpsed the big top on the common ground known as The Cloffocks on the other side of the river. Henry loved the circus, but it would not linger long and Matilda would hate for him to miss it. Would it be wrong to take him to see trapeze artists, clowns and performing seals before they checked their mother's grave? The weeds would not have grown *too* much over the winter.

As they continued north along the coast road, Matilda shivered in her thin frock. As the cab turned onto progressively narrower country lanes, her mouth dried.

When they pulled up at a pair of ornate wrought-iron gates and, in response to a blast of the horn, a man in a peaked cap emerged from a cottage on the other side to open them, Matilda realised she had underestimated the tradesman. He must be important to supply the grand estates.

The cab trundled up a tree-lined driveway and stopped outside a red-brick building with an imposing clock tower. When the men got out, and the driver opened her door and gestured for her to exit the taxi too, Matilda had a sense of being cast into one of Mrs Christie's murder mysteries. But none of the roles – victim, sleuth or socialite – seemed to fit.

When the tradesman offered Matilda his arm, Sister Bernadette remained in her seat. Whispering her prayers, her gaze inward, the nun looked as remote as a statue of the Virgin Mary. Matilda could not interrupt her devotions to ask her to intercede. It was all too clear that she would not be seeing her brother today. She would not be going home.

Her legs wobbled as the tradesman escorted her up the stone steps and a revolving door deposited her in a teak-lined vestibule. She caught a whiff of something sour, like nappies soaking in bleach. After setting down her case on the tiled floor, the cabbie withdrew.

At the sound of approaching footsteps, Matilda straightened her spine. The nuns might perceive this as her penance, but she would show her new employer she was unafraid of hard work. There was no shame in service. Some of her friends had toiled as maids since the age of thirteen.

Yet the odour of excrement and disinfectant prompted Matilda to reconsider. Perhaps the mansion hosted a training school for nannies, not a wealthy family and their staff. Matilda stood taller. Although no doubt inferior to the London college she had been promised, there were compensations in staying local. She could visit her brother at weekends.

A woman emerged from the gloom. She wore a stony expression and a starched white apron over a navy-blue dress. "Miss Osborne?"

Matilda nodded. The woman did not give her name. Or her position, but a tailored jacket and skirt would be more appropriate attire for a college principal.

"Pick up your case and come with me."

Matilda did not move. She recalled the warning quotation from Dante's Inferno: *Abandon hope all ye who enter here*. "What is this place?" She had no desire to acquire a reputation for defiance, but she had a right to know.

"Ghyllside is a hospital."

"Am I to be a nurse?"

Sniggering, the tradesman strode past her to shake the hand of a man whose face was deep in shadow.

"A patient."

"But I'm in perfect health." A little under par, but a few days' convalescence would rectify that. A week's at most.

"Ghyllside is a *mental* hospital," said the woman.

In the schoolyard, it was always other children – the slow kids, the barefoot kids, the kids whose mothers didn't have a penny for the public bathhouse on Friday nights – who were taunted. Told they belonged in the asylum. Her brother needed *her* at home. "There must be some mistake."

"That's what they all say." The woman rolled her eyes. "If you're not a mental case, why are you clad in a flimsy summer frock in the middle of March?"

Panic rising, Matilda spun around. There was her suitcase. Where was her coat? "I'm to be committed for forgetting my coat in the taxi?" She would fetch it and prove her sanity, unless they had already driven away. She pushed against the doors, but could not make them budge.

"Enough of the dramatics, Matilda."

The familiar male voice made her blood freeze. When the ice cracked, it would splinter her heart. "Father?" The man who ought to protect her would have her silenced. He had threatened as much but she never suspected he would act on it, if only for the sake of his son.

"I'm not mad," Matilda appealed to the woman she now deduced must be the matron. "Believe me, please."

The woman made no reply. She simply stared. Following her gaze, Matilda noticed that one of the white spots on her dress appeared irregular, not woven into the fabric but newly formed: a leakage from her breast.

"We also accommodate moral defectives," said the tradesman, as he bent to seize her case.

Matilda did not waste a moment asking what that meant. She sprang towards her stepfather and grabbed the lapels of his jacket. He smelled of shaving soap and pipe tobacco. "Please don't leave me here," she sobbed. "I'll be good, I'll do anything you want me to, if you'll have me home." When begging did not reach him, desperation sent her screeching, screaming and clawing at his clothes.

A shove, a slap and Matilda lay sprawled on the floor, her cheek stinging. Through a haze of tears she watched the tradesman unlock the revolving doors. She watched the man she had called her father pass through them without a backward glance.

Chapter 2: June, 1964

At the swish of the revolving doors, Matty retreats to the corner. When a student steps into the lobby, closely followed by another, she presses against the wood-panelled wall. The girls link arms, their starched white caps kissing as they lean close to continue the conversation paused by their divided entry. Matty tries to make herself invisible as she listens in.

One is telling the other about last night's antics at the staff social club. Everyone thought Jackie was on nights, but she turned up at last orders and caught her fiancé canoodling with Joanne. Nobody believed Josie when she said her shift dress was Mary Quant; besides, it looked ridiculous with those chubby thighs. They giggle. Matty wonders if she's met any of the three Js but, if there's a Jackie, Joanne or Josie on Ward 24, Matty knows only her surname.

As the nurses saunter past, their rubber-soled shoes squeaking on the tiled floor, Matty detects a snip of red lining dangling below the hem of one girl's black cape. Matron has reduced staff to tears for less. Matty calls out, "Miss!" When they continue walking, she raises her voice, "Nurse!"

They separate and turn around. One shakes her head. The other puts her hands on her hips. "Excuse me, we were talking. Don't you know it's rude to interrupt?"

"Yes, but ..." Matty points, but they have moved on.

Before they disappear up the corridor, one tosses a final remark over her shoulder. "If you need something, go to your ward. We're not on duty for another ten minutes."

Matty picks at the cracked leather of her handbag. Then she opens it and pops a jelly baby in her mouth. She sucks away the sugary shell before chewing the body.

Another nurse arrives: a man in a white tunic, grey trousers and no cloak. "Henry?" she whispers.

"Not me." He looks directly at her and winks, but doesn't tarry. "You asked me yesterday and the day before. If I didn't know better, I'd think you fancied me."

Cheeks roasting, Matty stares at her shoes. She can't decide which is worse: the staff who put up barriers or those who pretend those barriers don't exist. It was simpler in the old days.

But harsher, her mother reminds her. *Things you would not want a child to see.*

But now he is an adult, her brother *could* take a job at Ghyllside. If his constitution is strong enough. If he declines his claim on his father's business. Or he could manage the shop and come to Ghyllside on a Sunday or an evening midweek. He could come in cricket whites to bat or bowl against the staff team or in a modern suit and tie to dance with Jackie, Joanne or Josie at the social club. If he did, how would Matty recognise him after twenty-five years? She still pictures him as a boy of six.

She will not let such concerns spoil this special day. Matty's ward is going on an outing: a magical mystery tour.

Before that, she must rehearse. When the vestibule is clear of people, and the telephonist in her cubbyhole is preoccupied with her switchboard, Matty creeps towards the revolving doors. Inhaling deeply, she nudges the rightmost door until both edges of the quadrant are perfectly aligned with the frame. Exhaling, she steps back.

Let us inspect the weather, says her mother. Thus encouraged, Matty enters the space and pushes the metal bar. The compartment advances, and Matty toddles with it, the brush-rimmed verticals making a satisfying shush.

When open air supplants the curved walls, Matty stops pushing and stands before the outside world. Although blinkered by the stone columns flanking the door frame, Matty savours the view. Immediately below her, a carriage width from the bottom step, a magnificent rose bed encircles the flagpole. Behind it, across the main drive, sunlight sparkles on the ranks of windscreens in the car park. To the left, the chapel's stumpy turret overlooks the remains of the orchard and the kitchen garden returned to nature by government decree. To the right, beyond the red-brick doctors' residence, deckchairs are stacked on the veranda of the timber sports-pavilion awaiting the next match. Swapping her handbag from the crook of her left elbow to the right, Matty doubts the panorama is more magnificent from the steps of Buckingham Palace.

Shall we go farther? says her mother. Matty totters into a wider view: the three-storey nurses' home at ten of the clock;

the tennis courts at two. But, still sheltered by the portico, she cannot smell the roses. She cannot feel the breeze.

When she transfers her weight onto one leg to lift the other, Matty cannot go forward. She can only sway. It is most irregular: as if, although her brain wants to descend to the grounds, her body has lost the will to walk. Is this another side-effect of her morning medication? Her mother is strangely silent on the matter.

Matty returns to the foyer. Lowering her rump onto the wooden bench, she considers whether, once she has recuperated, she ought to make another attempt. If the social worker books her a bed in a hostel, Matty will need to be proficient in crossing the threshold unaccompanied. Yet, hostel places being so scarce, Matty could be in her dotage before a vacancy arises. She shudders. How dreadful to grow old in Ghyllside.

It will not come to that. Matty will recover her courage. Today's charabanc trip will assist that recovery. She does not anticipate any difficulties on the mystery tour: her feet would not dare defy the nurses. A successful outing will inspire her to venture outdoors alone.

Matty opens her handbag to examine her purse, first extracting her comb, her prayer book and the bag of jelly babies to get at it. She counts seven ha'pennies, a threepenny bit, three florins, a reddish-brown ten-bob note and a green one-pound note with the portrait of Queen Elizabeth. More than sufficient for ice cream, a souvenir for herself and one for the boy if something suitable catches her eye. Impossible to plan in more detail when their destination is a surprise.

Matty is stuffing her mouth with jelly babies, while replacing the rest of her belongings in her handbag, when she hears the revolving door swishing. She looks up as Doris lumbers into the lobby. She wears a faded tea dress and her usual tweed waistcoat armoured with enamel badges, sacred medals and lucky charms.

"There you are! You realise you've missed breakfast? Sister wouldn't save you none but I sneaked out a bowl of cornflakes and a cup of tea and hid them in my locker." Doris's metalwork tinkles as she limps across. Matty smells damp bath towels as Doris grabs her arm and yanks her to her feet. "Come on! The coach'll be here soon."

Following her friend up the corridor, Matty wonders how it would feel to link arms and lean in, bartering scandalous gossip. But what could she trade? She knows nothing about Jackie, Josie or Joanne. If they pop into the patients' dances, it's on the way to somewhere better, and to clear the floor when they demonstrate the jive.

Mounting the stairs to Ward 24, Matty's stomach rumbles, hungry for her bowl of soggy cornflakes and cup of cold tea. But, on reaching the dayroom en route to the dormitories, an extraordinary sight tempts her to linger. A nurse flits from chair to chair, dispensing cigarettes to every smoker, not from their personal supply but from the plastic tub reserved for behaviour-therapy rewards. Although the clock confirms it is not due for another hour, another nurse trots back and forth to a trolley to deliver cups of tea.

"Come in, ladies," Sister calls from beside the radiogram. "We're just about to start."

Matty finds a seat and accepts a cup of sweetened milky tea. She coughs as the woman in the adjoining chair blows smoke in her face.

"I have bad news, I'm afraid," says Sister. "The outing we were so looking forward to has been cancelled. Our driver has had a crash. They've taken him to the West Cumberland and the coach is a write-off. I'm so sorry to disappoint you."

Some patients groan. One starts to weep. Most simply suck on their cigarettes.

"Can we go tomorrow, then?" says Doris.

"We will try to rearrange," says Sister. "But it won't be tomorrow, no. That's far too short notice."

"Next week?" Doris asks.

"More likely September or October," says Sister. "After the staff summer holiday period."

"But ..." Doris unclips a German St Christopher from the breast pocket of her waistcoat and pokes the pin beneath her thumbnail.

"Now, I know I can trust you ladies not to make a fuss." Sister sails towards the nurses' station where the picture window overlooks the lounge. "Let's make the best of things, shall we? If we have a nice peaceful morning, we might have a picnic in the grounds this afternoon." With a smile, Sister enters the office and closes the door.

The nurses collect cups and saucers. The wanderers leave their seats to pace the room. Matty slips into a newly vacated chair beside Doris, who swings her good leg back and forth as if to kick a ball. Or Sister's derriere.

"A picnic," says Matty. Determined to make the best of things, she hopes for egg-and-cress and shrimp-paste sandwiches in soft, white, bridge rolls. There might even be fizzy lemonade. Unfortunately, the hospital shop, where she buys her jelly babies, does not stock souvenirs.

The woman seated on Doris's other side leans across her. "I wonder where we'll have it." Clara wears pink-framed spectacles with smudgy lenses. "The swimming pool would be bliss." She covers her mouth at the audacity of suggesting patients invade staff facilities.

You must beware of sunburn, says Matty's mother. *You're particularly susceptible on those pills.*

Matty nods. Doris paints a trail of blood along her bare arm with her pierced thumb. "I've half a mind to dance on their immaculate cricket pitch. That would learn them."

"Would you do that new dance?" says Matty. "The twist." She has not yet attempted the peculiar gyrations. It seems pitiful to cavort without a gentleman's embrace. *That explains the origin of that lament by The Spiders: "I want to hold your hand".*

Clara untucks her blouse from the waistband of her skirt to wipe her spectacles. When she returns them to her face, the lenses are no cleaner. "Personally, I don't see the point of the circus."

"I like the elephants," says Doris.

Matty likes all the acts but, as far as she can recall, there is no dancing. There are pirouettes and sparkly leotards, acrobats and leaping lions, but no foxtrot or waltz.

"So it's no skin off my nose if it's cancelled."

She is mistaken, says Matty's mother. *Her nose is peeling. Excess exposure to the sun.*

Doris snorts. "You think they were taking us to the circus?"

"I *know* they were."

"Give over," says Doris. "It was a *mystery* tour."

"Well, someone knew where we were going," says Clara.

"Yeah, the bus driver," says Doris. "I suppose you've got a direct line to his hospital bed?"

The correct word is telepathy, says Matty's mother.

"Sister would know," says Matty. She would have to approve its suitability for her ladies.

"And she must've told that student with the squinty eye," says Clara. "'Cause *she* put up a poster for Billy Smart's in the dining room after breakfast. Said the walls needed brightening up."

"She never," says Doris.

"Cross my heart, Billy Smart's at The Cloffocks," says Clara. "Check for yourself if you don't believe me."

The Cloffocks, says Matty's mother. *What fun we used to have. I haven't thought of it for years.*

"Come on!" Matty springs from her seat and dashes towards the dining room. Clara follows at a more leisurely pace. Doris trails behind, dragging her gammy leg.

With no nurse in sight to prevent her, Matty barges into the room. The circus poster is immediately apparent, flanked by a black-and-white image of a young man with guitar and harmonica, and an uninspiring advert for the Tokyo Olympic Games. "Billy Smart's Circus, the greatest show on earth." The venue, the date and a picture of a chimpanzee banging a drum, amusingly attired in a ringmaster's top hat, bow tie and red jacket. "Damn that driver. Why did he have to crash?"

Doris comes and stands beside her. "We can still go."

"Sister said September or October," says Matty. "It will be gone by then."

"It'll be gone by tomorrow." Clara jabs the poster with a nicotine-stained finger. "Today's the last day."

Matty flops onto the nearest chair, beside a table set for luncheon with beakers for water and aluminium knives, forks and spoons.

"So we'd best get our skates on," says Doris.

"Sister said ..." says Matty.

"We don't need the nurses," says Doris. "We can go by ourselves."

"Sister wouldn't let us." Matty picks up a knife with GHYLLSIDE HOSPITAL stamped on the handle.

"Sister can't stop us," says Doris. "We're *informal* now."

That might be so, thinks Matty. But the formal approach is more efficient. "Do *you* know how to hire a coach?"

Clara laughs. "No need. You'd catch the bus from the bottom of the drive. Like normal people."

"You'll come, then, Clara?" says Doris.

"Not me. I told you, it's not my cup of tea. The clowns give me the heebie-jeebies and the animals stink."

"Right, Matty. It's you and me."

Matty takes a fork in her left hand to balance the knife in her right. Excitement versus security, how can she choose? She would love the circus, but she has not left Ghyllside unescorted in twenty-five years. "Maybe tomorrow."

"It'll be over tomorrow," says Clara. "It's now or never."

Doris snatches the cutlery and lays it on the table. "I'm not gonna beg, Matty. If you won't come with me, I'll go on my tod."

Doris has placed the knife on the right and the fork on the left. Matty swaps them around.

Chapter 3: March, 1939

My darling brother,

I am sorry I could not be with you this Christmas, but I trust you have been a good boy for Father and Santa brought you lots of presents.

Life is full of surprises. The stork brought a friend an unexpected delivery and I have been caring for her ever since. My friend's brother is thrilled to become an uncle. I am sure you would make a splendid uncle too when the time comes.

So please excuse the delay to my homecoming. I will be back at The Willows as soon as I can. Be a brave little soldier for me, Henry, and remember me in your prayers.

Your loving sister,

Tilly.

If only she had a stamp to send it. But Matilda cannot even scavenge a pad and pen.

The matron, along with the man Matilda mistook for a tradesman, hauled her along a corridor, up some stairs and into a room with five bathtubs. *He* took her suitcase and left; *she* took three inches of Matilda's hair, exposing her ears and neck, and told her to strip and get in the bath. The nearest held a shallow span of grimy water, but when Matilda sidled to an empty one, the matron called her back. When she went to pull the plug, the matron barred her way. "Get in the bath, you trollop."

Matilda began to shake. "It's dirty."

"And so are you."

She told herself she did not need the woman's good opinion. Just as she had told herself she did not need to please the nuns. But she was wrong on both counts. The matron would not leave the room until she stepped into the chill, grey water.

Matilda did not object to bathing: a warm bath might ease the aches from her fall in the vestibule; a clean bath might help heal her postpartum wounds. But this was neither. As soon as she heard the key turn in the door as the matron left, Matilda climbed out, planting wet footprints on the cork mat.

Throughout the trials of her teenage years, Matilda had found comfort in remembering her mother. She would talk to her in her mind; not quite conversation, but more immediate than prayer. Although, naturally, she could not *hear* any reply, Matilda *sensed* her mother's guidance. So now, imagining her mother recommending she dress and await the opportunity to explain the situation to some higher authority, Matilda felt calmer. Until she realised her clothes had disappeared. Then she made herself numb and, when fear bubbled up in her, she forced it down, became a statue, cold as marble. Ghyllside could not be any worse than the nunnery, and she had survived that. Things would improve when she met the other girls. This purgatory could not persist forever.

She was seated on a stool, naked and shivering, when the door opened and a nurse, who looked no older than Matilda herself, dropped a basket of mud-coloured cloth at her feet. "Get dressed!"

Summoning the dregs of her dignity, Matilda stood and extended her hand. "Pleased to meet you. I'm Matilda and you are – ?"

"Very busy. So look lively."

Matilda found some underwear in the basket. Her skin crawled as she dragged on someone else's bloomers and petticoat, but she would be better equipped to enquire about her own clothes if she was half decent. "There's been a mistake. These aren't mine."

"You'll wear what you're given."

Like at the convent, although the girls' baggy smocks served a purpose there. "Thank you, but I don't need charity. I brought a suitcase of cardigans, skirts and blouses, but it seems to have been mislaid. A gentleman took it and the lady must have taken the frock I was wearing. Red, with white spots."

"You'll get it Friday."

"Thank you, but please don't go to any trouble. It does not require laundering. I can rinse the stain from the bodice at the sink."

"*It does not require laundering.*" The girl mimicked Matilda's elocution-class vowels. "You'll get a shock when you find there's no servants at your beck and call."

Matilda rose above the juvenile spitefulness. "I expect to be gone by Friday. I would hate to waste your time."

"Move your arse. That's *my* seat."

Matilda jolted from a dreamland, where circus clowns regaled her mother and brother, to the nightmare of an asylum ward. It was Friday and her frock had not been returned to her. *She* had not been returned to The Willows.

Despite repeated requests, she had not seen a doctor. Instead, she was roused from her narrow iron bed at an ungodly hour to slave in the bakery. The noise, the heat and the lacklustre product scuttled her already sinking spirits. But starting work before dawn had one advantage: finishing earlier than the kitchen assistants and laundresses meant a brief respite from the groans, shrieks and nonsensical prattle of the pitiable creatures among whom she was billeted.

She had hoped to use the quiet to order her thoughts. Although she had yet to secure the materials to do so, Matilda felt desperate to write to her brother. The impossibility of explaining to a six-year-old how his unmarried sister had had a baby had prevented her writing from the convent. But this further delay to her homecoming, even if only for another week, would be hard for the child to bear. Matilda was the closest to a mother Henry had known.

Yet in the space of three days she had become so estranged from how her brother perceived her, her mind was a muddle. Exhausted from her labours, both delivering the baby and now in the bake-house, depleted by pregnancy and a starvation diet, confused and despondent about her circumstances, it was a blessed relief to drift into oblivion. Yet how would she regain her freedom if she did not fight? She had accepted the loss of her baby. She must not lose her self.

On the day she arrived, when the young nurse who mocked her diction led her from the bathroom to the refectory, Matilda pinned her hopes on the community of detainees. She swallowed her disappointment that nobody replied when she introduced herself more easily than she swallowed the gristly stew that passed for supper. Perched on the wooden bench at the end of a long table, she watched the women slurp their victuals, fending off incursions with their arms around their plates. She watched them lick the chipped crockery when they were finished and listened to them belch and chunter to themselves. She wondered who would befriend her when they retired to the dormitory and were finally unobserved. In the home for unwed mothers, the nuns controlled their tongues in the daytime, but the nights belonged to them. She might find *less* support from the certified lunatics than the fallen women, but Matilda trusted she would find *some*.

Yet when she spoke, no one answered. When she shook her neighbour by the shoulder, the patient looked afraid and turned away. In the moonlight flooding the dormitory, the women stared at Matilda with slack mouths and empty eyes.

Move your arse. That's my seat. Despite the shapeless frock that betrayed her lowly status, the speaker seemed too substantial to be a patient. Too menacing. As if the scraps of tin pinned to her bodice were military medals. As if the wooden crutch she leant on were a musket and not a mobility aid.

Matilda's gaze swept the ranks of unoccupied chairs, differing solely in their placement, as far as she could tell. Her chair afforded neither a window view onto parkland nor a secluded hideaway from the staff. Did it have some arcane value to the disturbed mind?

"Didn't you hear me? Shove off!"

What would her mother advise? It did not do to pander to bullies, but Matilda was weary. She had to conserve her strength for the serious battles.

As she trudged towards a seat at the opposite end of the room, the madwoman called after her, "I run this ward, new girl. And don't you forget it."

When grace was said at the end of the evening meal, Matilda braced herself for a few hours of tedium before bedtime. But instead of being marched back to the ward in single file, as on previous occasions, a nurse escorted the patients from the dining hall in groups of half a dozen. Anticipating some new form of torture, when Matilda's turn came, she gripped the table as the taste of black pudding and Cumberland sausage tickled her throat.

"You can stop that gurning," said the nurse. "Or Sister won't let you go to the dance."

"Dance?" The word must have another meaning in Ghyllside.

"Aye, it's Friday, isn't it? Away and get your glad rags on."

Matilda fingered the bristles at her nape where the matron had cropped her hair. But the horrors of the last few days had pushed her beyond vanity. Looking frowzy was a small price to pay for seeing her friends at the Stanley Hall. They would get a message to Henry. They would help her escape.

She would feel more like herself in her own clothes. More able to think. Her polka-dot dress could mask a multitude of miseries.

The nurse herded them into the dormitory where a clothes rack displayed a variety of frocks suspended from a rail. "Help yourselves, ladies."

The rainbow hues were as glorious as the first film in Technicolor after black and white. Rattling the hangers back and forth, Matilda homed in on the reds.

She turned to the nurse. "My frock isn't here."

The nurse barely raised her head from fastening the buttons on an apricot rayon. "Then choose another."

"You don't understand." Matilda tugged at the nurse's sleeve. "It's my own frock. The one I came in."

The nurse shook her off. "I don't think *you* understand, Miss High and Mighty. The dance dresses are for everyone. Don't be so possessive."

A patient in ill-fitting lilac crêpe tapped her shoulder. "It's for the best. We can wear summat different each week."

Across the room, women sat on their beds, like wind-up toys waiting for someone to turn the key. The only one in motion was applying lipstick to a fellow patient's mouth. Matilda was determined not to stoop to sharing cosmetics. The scene made a poor parody of those Fridays in Hilda's bedroom, getting dolled up to meet Walter and Bert at the Stanley Hall.

How foolish to imagine pitching up there. How foolish to count on seeing her friends. There would be other ballrooms closer to Ghyllside.

What did it matter where they went and what she wore as long as the floor was properly sprung? Matilda would waltz away her woes in a gentleman's arms. As she steeled herself to approach the rail of communal gowns, a flash of pillar-box red dotted with white snagged her gaze.

She had conceded to the bully with the crutch once already. She would not surrender a second time. Not when she had filched Matilda's favourite frock *and* punctured the fabric to attach her makeshift medals.

Chapter 4: June, 1964

Matty learnt about the changes to the regulations regarding psychiatric patients similarly to how she learnt about the changes in the female body from girl to woman: in dribs and drabs of truth, distortions and outright lies. No one explained the implications: firstly thinking her too innocent, then assuming she must know. So she hurtled from ignorance to experience without a guiding hand.

The work in the hospital bakery became less arduous. Then it stopped altogether, with the bread for their morning toast delivered from outside. Then, after several weeks of idleness, work started up again, except now it was called Industrial Therapy, where they were paid for their labour, or Occupational Therapy, where they were not. Although Matty does not miss the heat, noise and pre-dawn starts, she takes no pride in assembling Christmas crackers in August or packing bite-sized chocolate eggs in cellophane in November.

Patients no longer trooped to the huge refectory at mealtimes; instead, smaller dining rooms were carved out on individual wards. One day, Matty returned from a macramé session to find a small closet beside her bed in the dormitory. The following day, she discovered a handbag perched upon it, which the nurse insisted belonged to her. Given the tarnished white leather, Matty was sceptical, but, having no other, she took it under her wing. But, when a brown suitcase appeared, she could not bring herself to open it and toed it under her bed.

Was it before or after this that the patients' drab uniform dresses were retired? A lady from the sewing room carried a catalogue from patient to patient and invited them to choose not one new outfit but three. An occupational therapist provided everyone with needles, thread and woven name tapes to prevent their clothes going astray. They even personalised their underwear; a godsend given the ghastly condition of the bloomers issued to Matty in the past. Loose elastic being the least of her concerns.

If Matty had paused to wonder what prompted these developments, she would have attributed them to the whim of a new matron or medical superintendent. She could not imagine parliamentarians stooping to debate the mental hospital regime. Yet they must have done so to pass a law that relaxed the rules. Snatches of overheard conversations proved the nurses grasped the detail no more firmly than the patients, but they surmised the government sought revolution, not reform.

Unlocking the ward doors seemed radical enough until it emerged that the health minister had pledged to abolish the long-stay hospitals altogether. Some were delighted, others alarmed and several on both sides doubted it would happen. What did politicians know about psychiatry? Staff or patient, everyone had to find their balance between hopes and fears for the future, between inertia and haste.

When asked her opinion on graduating from Ghyllside to a hostel, Matty felt like a child forced to grow up too quickly. Naturally, she could not decline such an opportunity, but she wished it would not arise too soon. She was scared that losing her patienthood would be as drastic as losing her virginity, the consequences as dire. So, when no hostel place materialised, she felt grateful for the comfort of something positive to aim for without disturbing the status quo.

Now the pace is speeding up again. If only Clara had not mentioned the circus. If only the student nurse had not taped that blasted poster to the wall.

Perhaps Doris shares her regrets. She peels away the bottom corners and rips the flyer from the wall. "Bloody provocation." She folds it in half, in quarters, in eighths and thrusts it in her waistcoat pocket. "Rubbing our noses in what we're missing."

"I thought you were going anyroad," says Clara.

"I am." Doris casts Matty a furtive glance.

Matty squirms. It would be more manageable with the three of them. Or two, excluding her. "You might enjoy the trapeze artists, Clara. Or you might meet an old flame."

"*You* might meet an old flame," says Doris. "Aren't you from that neck of the woods?"

Matty swaps the knife and fork back over again. Dare she hope to bump into her brother? Dare she ring the doorbell of the house where he was born?

"Well, I'd best get cracking." Doris does not move. "You never know, if I like it round them parts, I might not bother coming back."

"Give over," says Clara. "Where will you sleep? A park bench?"

Matty stays quiet, but Doris has her sympathy. She feels it too: the sense that, if she leaves the hospital grounds, she'll be exiled.

What a conundrum! says her mother. *Thankfully, the decision is out of your hands.* Matty need not worry about disappointing Doris. She need not worry about revisiting old haunts. Much as her eyes would love to see the circus, her legs will not allow her to exit the building. Her body is beyond her mind's control.

Chapter 5: March/April, 1939

My darling brother,

I am sorry about the further delay to my homecoming. Silly me, I was out in the rain without a coat or umbrella and caught a chill. Now I am convalescing but should be back at The Willows before too long. I am being well looked after with lots of hearty meals and fresh air. It would be like a holiday if not for missing you. Father will think me quite spoilt when I return.

Be a brave little soldier and wait a little longer, Henry, and remember me in your prayers as I remember you in mine.

Your loving sister,

Tilly.

—ell—

Matilda did not get to the dance that Friday. But neither did the bully. Something snapped when she saw that creature parading in her polka-dot dress. All the hurts and humiliations of her childhood and teens hardened her hands into fists. Matilda's mother would have been ashamed of her. But if her mother had not left her an orphan, Matilda would not have had to fight.

Despite her bruises, Matilda had the best night's sleep in several weeks. But, the following morning, the cushioned walls of the seclusion room closed in on her. In the silence, she thought she could hear her pulse. Without a watch, and with only a tiny window too near the ceiling to permit a view of the grounds, she had no means of measuring time. But her bladder was fit to burst when the nurse brought her breakfast tray. As she led Matilda to the stinking lavatories, the nurse did not utter a word.

After a second night in isolation, Matilda rejoiced when they collected her for church on Sunday morning. However, Ghyllside having its own chapel, she could escape her cell but she could not escape the grounds. Still tender from the beating, she scanned the pews for the woman with the crutch. Finding no sign of her, Matilda sang "Now Thank We All Our God" with extra vigour.

On a second survey of the congregation, she almost dropped her hymnbook. Ghyllside imprisoned men as well as women: row upon row of them sat across the aisle in shabby mud-brown suits. Matilda smoothed her shapeless dress and patted her irregular coiffeur.

Chancing a third glance, Matilda caught her breath. Although identically clad, one fellow stood out from his peers. His proud deportment suggested a superior status; his exotic roots evident in his chocolate-coloured skin. Her brain buzzed with questions. Why had he come to Cumberland? From what country did he hail?

Turning her head a fourth time, she felt her arm wrenched. Matilda trembled as the matron lugged her outdoors.

The woman wagged a finger in her face. "I'm watching you, strumpet. And if you're planning any hanky-panky, I'll have you sterilised."

Without completely understanding either accusation or warning, Matilda sensed both were undesirable. And, like the hacking of her hair, undeserved.

The following day, it was back to the bakery, until an assistant interrupted Matilda's work to summon her to see the doctor. At last! She could barely coordinate her fingers to unfasten her floury apron.

After the heat of the ovens, the consulting room seemed chilly, but Matilda thought she detected some warmth in the doctor's demeanour. Surely an educated man would rectify the matron's folly.

Seated behind a desk in a double-breasted pinstripe suit with matching waistcoat, he appraised Matilda over the top of his half-moon spectacles. Fearing he would consider her forward if she spoke first, Matilda waited, tugging at her hair.

"You've caused your family a great deal of trouble, Miss Osborne. I hope you'll be more amenable here."

Despite the content of his speech, Matilda felt encouraged by his delivery. Like hers, his accent was polished. "I don't know why I'm here, sir. Or how long I must stay."

He did not rush to reply, as if taking a soothing stroll through the pathways of his brain to pluck his words like blossom from a bush. "That rather depends on you."

"I can go when I please?" She had already wasted a week in this snake pit.

His lips twitched, as if she were a child asking to choose her own bedtime. "You can go when you've proved you've ceased to be a risk."

Matilda pressed her palms against her legs to stop them quivering. "In what way am *I* a risk?"

The doctor made a great show of studying the file in front of him. "You attacked a fellow patient last Friday. Assaulted your father the minute you walked through our doors." His tone was neutral; the facts themselves condemned her.

"I was distraught." Sensing a similar rage now rising from her belly, Matilda squashed it down. She imagined her mother's arm around her shoulders, whispering in her ear. *Keep calm, my precious. The doctor will be kind if you tell him the truth.* "That man conspired to have me locked up."

"Conspired?" The doctor unscrewed the cap from his fountain pen.

Through the consulting-room window, Matilda thought she glimpsed the dark gentleman from the chapel. She blinked, and the man digging the bare earth in his shirt sleeves and braces turned white. Was her mind playing tricks on her after another sleepless night, or did they drug the patients' tea? "I'm here under false pretences. I am perfectly sane."

The doctor's pen-nib scratched the page. When it stopped, he looked up. "With respect, Miss Osborne, you're in no position to judge. Allow me to clarify a potential misconception ..."

Confident he could not justify her incarceration, but conscious of her obligation to hear him out, Matilda wriggled in her seat and pushed her fists under her thighs.

"The brain is a complex organ, Miss Osborne, its defects manifest in myriad ways. For some – the idiots, imbeciles and feeble-minded – it shows in arrested development. For some, disordered mood – despondency, apathy or excess jollity – brings mental torture. In other tragic cases, perceptions are distorted – patients confuse fantasy with reality, they see and hear things that are not there. Finally, there are those who seem unremarkable on the surface, but conduct themselves in a morally reprehensible manner. Some criminals fall into this category, along with prostitutes, drunkards and unmarried mothers."

"I'm being punished for ..." She cannot name it, or not to this man who, for all his polite placidity, despises her as much as *she* despises murderers and thieves.

"Not punished as such, but segregated, yes, as all who pose a threat to common decency must be. But it isn't so bad here. You'll grow accustomed to our ways."

Did the doctor notice her staring at the sheaf of foolscap by his telephone? Did he see her gazing greedily at the inkwell and the blotter splodged with black? "I do appreciate it isn't easy initially," he said. "If there's anything I can do to help you acclimatise ..."

Matilda gulped. "If I might have pen and paper to write to my brother."

"I'm afraid that is out of the question."

"But I promised him I'd come home again. He won't understand why I haven't. He'll miss me dreadfully. He's only six."

"Such an impressionable age."

"It is."

"Which makes it essential we protect him from corruption. Fortunately, he's young enough to forget you."

Not yet twenty and her life over, Matilda would not give them the gratification of seeing her weep. Or hearing her. But, with privacy a scarce commodity at Ghyllside, she was forced to smother her grief. She could not hide in the lavatories when the cubicles had neither locks nor doors; besides, the stench would have intensified her suffering. She could not retreat to the dormitory in the daytime, with entry barred from early morning until after cocoa at seven o'clock. She could have added her voice to the chorus of nocturnal wailing, but Matilda's melancholy deserved a solo. *Her* lament had meaning; the madwomen's moans were hollow babble.

She buried her face in her pillow and when she awoke, convinced she had not slept, the cotton was damp. She crawled through the week, still alert for potential enemy sightings; no longer to avoid an altercation, but in hope the bully's crutch would finish her off.

When Friday came, and no one else picked Matilda's polka-dot dress, it seemed easier to put it on and go where she was directed than to protest she was in no mood to dance. Now, when no charabanc arrived to drive them to a proper dance hall and instead they were marched, crocodile fashion, down an interminable corridor, Matilda felt relieved to be shielded from the society that shunned her. She could not have stomached so stark a reminder of her loss.

Her first sight of Ghyllside's ballroom was so shocking, she could only laugh. She gazed about her, stock still, such that the patient in line behind her jabbed her in the back. On a stage framed by a mosaic of gladioli, eight or nine musicians were tuning their instruments. Chandeliers illuminated the brightly tiled walls and the stained glass in some of the windows. If it did not reach the standard of the famous ballroom at Blackpool Tower, where she had first worn her polka-dot dress, it came close. Matilda looked forward to testing the floor.

The presence of men completed the sense of awe. They sat on one side of the room, the women on the other. Matilda tapped her foot as soon as the band launched their repertoire, but, unsure of the etiquette in a mental hospital, she held back. At Blackpool, she had stood up with another girl until two men claimed them, but now, when she gestured to a potential female partner, the nurse waved her away. Seemingly, they were not permitted initiative even at a dance.

Instead, a nurse acted as matchmaker: summoning a lady from one side and a gentleman from the other and manoeuvring their arms into position. When she saw how clumsily some of them danced, Matilda accepted the regimentation would prevent an injury to the feebler patients. Also, the nurses could ensure that even the most withdrawn would have a chance. Although frustrated at having to wait, Matilda tried to hang onto the chip of cheerfulness that had struck her on entering the ballroom. She would pass the time trying to make eye contact with the coloured man she had seen in the chapel. Was he African? American? Did he speak English? Did he know how to dance?

She did not think her attraction was romantic; she did not think she could ever be romantically involved again. But he was like her – an anomaly in this place – and therefore more fascinating than anyone else. Crossing her fingers, she prayed the nurse would bring them together.

When the music stopped, Matilda assumed it was an interval for refreshments. But no, the nurses assembled their charges, counted their heads and paraded them back to their various wards. They were leaving before the atmosphere had warmed sufficiently. They were leaving before Matilda had danced.

As they trooped towards the exit, another procession edged the same way. Naturally, the gentlemen paused to let the ladies through but, as they did, Matilda finally received a smile from her African prince. Next week they would dance together, even if she had to ask him herself.

Matilda had waited a week for this opportunity. As she approached the dark-skinned gentleman, however, panic seemed to flash across his face. She faltered but, glancing around, the nurse who had escorted her and the other ladies from her ward to Ghyllside's ballroom seemed unconcerned. Indeed, she looked to be *flirting* with a nurse from the male side.

Although *Matilda's* interest was purely fraternal, she took it as encouragement to proceed. "May I have this dance?"

Perspiration moistened her armpits when the fellow did not reply. Did he not speak English? Had she contravened some cultural taboo? Or perhaps he thought her too ugly with her pasty complexion and scarecrow hair.

"I ain't never been asked by a lady before," he drawled, eventually. His accent so strange, Matilda could not distinguish whether he admired or condemned her for flouting convention. His subsequent silence suggested the latter.

Red cheeked, she turned to the chap beside him, determined to dance before "Happy Days Are Here Again" petered out. "Would you care –"

Her invitation was unfinished when the coloured fellow stepped between them. "Begging your pardon, ma'am, been here so long I've mislaid my manners." He clasped her right hand with his left, his touch gentle despite the roughness of his skin. Her body responded automatically, her left arm resting on his right as his hand on her upper back steered her onto the floor. "I'm Eustace."

"Pleased to meet you. I'm Matilda."

"Do you like waltzing, Matilda?"

She laughed, although she had heard the joke so often the humour had waned. "I do."

The tune ended and they stepped apart to applaud the band. Matilda stood awkwardly as the floor cleared. Although Eustace did not leave her stranded, she wondered if he felt he had done his duty and half a dance should suffice. When the first notes of "Sing a Song of Sunbeams" spilled into the room, Matilda channelled their brightness into her voice, "I do like waltzing, but I much prefer the quickstep."

Eustace grinned. "Me too."

They cruised the ballroom, as finely matched as Ginger Rogers and Fred Astaire, although Eustace resembled Louis Armstrong and Matilda lacked Miss Rogers' luscious hair. "Where did you learn to dance?" she asked.

"Back home."

"America?"

"Not in the way you mean."

How did he know what she meant? Matilda was not sure herself. "Africa?"

"I'm a British subject. Same as you."

Had she offended him? She was only making conversation. There was no call to be contrary. "But not from Cumberland?" she tried. He did not answer.

When the music stopped, Matilda clapped so earnestly her palms stung. As did her eyes. If Eustace had tired of her, let him bear the consequences. She would not resume her seat willingly. He would have to tow her back to the ladies' side.

Perhaps he sensed her resolve because, as soon as the musicians commenced "The Blue Danube", he swept her into the waltz. "Let's see how long we can keep going before dem nurses split us up."

In that moment, Matilda yearned for her previous partners, who flattered her with charming words. But which of them would have kept their dignity in a madhouse, overseen by surly guards? Handsome and light on his feet, Eustace was the equal of any Englishman.

Sweat glistened on his forehead when the musicians put down their instruments. In her clumpy shoes, Matilda's arches were beginning to ache. A nurse blew a whistle to signal the patients to line up ward by ward. "Same next week?" said Eustace. "Assuming dem dictators don' interfere."

Whatever *his* motivation, Matilda was grateful for his embrace. Until he held her, her closest connection to another inmate came via a madwoman's crutch. "I'd be delighted. That's if I'm still here."

He chuckled. "I hope you're not, for your sake. But, if you are, be sure to wear dat pretty dress."

Chapter 6: June, 1964

She must be hallucinating. This can't be real. Yet Matty can feel the soles of her shoes skimming the tarmac, Doris's arm dragging on hers as they skip to an arrhythmic beat. She can feel her cheeks warming, by the sun from the outside and by her giddy amazement from within. She inhales the scent of the rose bushes, or perhaps she simply smells the absence of indoor staleness. She has to be dreaming. She is definitely awake.

Reaching the porter's lodge at the end of the drive, they slow their pace, as if fearing some invisible barrier between the stone gateposts will catapult them back to the ward. But nothing blocks them. They pass through the gap unopposed.

Releasing Matty's arm, Doris scans the road for the bus stop. She has begun to march towards it when she stalls and swings around to scrutinise Matty's face. "You're crying!" Her fingertip scrapes a tear from under Matty's eye.

"I didn't know," says Matty. How many times has she braved the revolving doors and circled back to the vestibule without venturing farther? How many hours has she wasted being a mere spectator, absorbing the view without daring to claim the stage? "I didn't know it would be so easy."

"Barmpot." Doris's arms wrap around her, squeezing them chest to chest.

Matty's sobbing intensifies. Nobody has held her like this since the home for unwed mothers a quarter of a century before.

Doris steps back. "I thought this were meant to be fun."

"I'll be fine, honestly." Matty pokes under her cardigan sleeve for her hanky.

Doris grasps her hand as a red double-decker trundles along the road. Waving frantically, they race towards it. The bus comes to a halt and they grab the pole at the rear to climb aboard. Matty would have liked to sit on top and look down on fields and farms, to strain her eyes for a glimpse of the sea. But she is no longer a girl and Doris would have struggled with the stairs.

They lurch down the aisle and collapse onto a bench seat. "Let me do the talking," says Doris, as the clippie approaches to take their fares.

Matty expects Doris to spin some story to explain their escape from the asylum, but she merely checks the bus is heading in the right direction. The clippie does not raise an eyebrow as she turns the handle of her ticket machine.

The price has increased since Matty last took a bus, but she has sufficient funds in her purse to pay for them both. Having set off in a hurry, Doris has neither purse nor handbag. Matty hopes the cash she counted earlier will cover their entries to the circus, the bus back to Ghyllside and a bite to eat. As anxiety retreats from her stomach, hunger moves in. She never got to eat the breakfast Doris saved for her and her jelly babies are gone.

When the clippie withdraws to assist another passenger off the bus, Doris leans close to Matty. "If anybody asks, you're a duchess and I'm your lady-in-waiting."

Matty giggles. "Me, a duchess?" Who would believe her? Who would care? She cannot envisage speaking to anyone except to buy tickets or a snack.

"An heiress, then."

You are heir to my affection, says her mother.

"We need to have summat ready. Else folk will wonder why a posh lass is mixing with a girl from the gutter."

You were born in a slum, says her mother.

"It is none of their business," says Matty. "But you may tell them whatever you wish." She would go along with anything that made her friend happy. Especially today, with the bonus of her mother's company. Is that an omen? On the few previous trips arranged by the staff, her mother stayed behind. Should Matty take her presence as a prompt to seek out Henry? If she did, she would have to do so unaccompanied – her brother might frown on her friend's rough manners – but she could not leave Doris alone.

What will be, will be, sings her mother. *Consider today a rehearsal. You will have other opportunities to reconnect once you are proficient in the art of mingling.*

Matty feels suddenly taller. If the driver had not crashed the charabanc, her freedom would have ended on returning to Ghyllside. The disappointment of the cancelled tour was the catalyst for greater independence. She and Doris can ride into town every week if they have the bus fare.

First they will practice. Then they will secure a room in a hostel. They will find jobs as shop girls. Or as secretaries, like in the films shown in Ghyllside's ballroom on Saturday nights. They will learn to love the latest fashions. They will go dancing, despite Doris's gammy leg.

One step at a time, her mother cautions. Breathless, as if from running to keep abreast with her mind's ambition, Matty appreciates the advice. She calms herself by gazing through the window. Although not high enough to spot the Solway Firth, she can see the Lakeland fells in the distance and meadows grazed by sheep and cows close by.

As the lanes turn to roads and the roads widen, more passengers board to fill the vacant seats. Matty's attention switches from pasture to people, farm animal to human. She tries not to stare, but they differ so much from the familiar, she could be abroad. Although several are bronzed by the sun, none are cocoa dark like Eustace, yet by their dress and deportment they appear more foreign than he ever seemed to be.

She has seen ladies in trousers before today, or in frocks that barely cover their buttocks. She has seen men wearing polo-neck sweaters under sports jackets instead of shirts and ties. But what seemed racy at Ghyllside – the garb of an off-duty nurse, or an actor on the big screen – is tame on this Cumbrian bus. Bold patterns in clashing colours dazzle her eyes and she blushes at the amount of exposed skin. Matty shrinks in her seat. In her pleated kilt, nylon cardigan and plain polyester blouse, she feels more country bumpkin than society heiress.

Above the growl of the engine and the onboard chatter, a whistle blows. On the right, a train draws level with the bus, then chugs away in a cloud of steam. Beyond the tracks, Matty catches her breath at the sight of water. Could they make time for a paddle? Bereft of her home, her friends and family, she had not realised she has also missed the sea.

As the road bends to the left, and the railway line shunts off towards the viaduct, Doris digs her elbow into Matty's ribs. Across the river, amid a sprawling encampment, is the distinctive red and white striped canvas of the circus tent. Despite committing to the venture less than an hour ago, Matty feels as if she has been travelling towards the big top all her life.

Nervous about finally arriving, and too self-conscious to get off before the other passengers, she does not tell Doris they could reach Billy Smart's in five minutes if the driver dropped them at the bus stop beside Navvies Bridge. But continuing to the town centre brings other complications. Almost next door to the bus station is Windsor's Haberdashery; will she spot her brother at work in his father's shop?

My darling brother,

I hope you are having a lovely summer. Mine would be perfect if not for missing you.

Do you remember Reginald, the Welsh gentleman we met at Blackpool? His mother invited me to convalesce at their farm. Now recovered from my illness, I feel obliged to repay her kindness and remain until harvest time. The work never ends in the countryside and the family appreciate an extra pair of hands. I have become quite brown from being outdoors all day. You would not believe the muscles in my arms.

I will be home as soon as I am able and we will have such fun together. Be a brave little soldier in the meantime, Henry, and remember me in your prayers.

Your loving sister,
Tilly.

———

Matilda's twentieth birthday passed without ceremony. Would she be free to leave when she came of age next year? Eustace had not gained his liberty and he was forty. Some patients appeared twice that or more.

She was shocked when she realised how old he must be. Although why should she care about the age difference? She had not considered him husband material. But, in the weeks since they met, she had come to treasure him as a friend.

Trudging single-file to the hospital chapel, or caged in the airing courts below the ward, the sun's heat continually surprised her when winter reigned perpetually indoors. Instead of marking time by the seasons, Matilda measured her wasted youth in a succession of Friday evenings. Excitement mounted as she accelerated towards them, mixed with anxiety Eustace would not attend or the bully would return to filch her polka-dot dress. She would shed her woes on entering the ballroom, surrendering her mind to the music, her feet to the dance. When it was over, she would plummet into desolation, with a seven-day wait to feel human again.

Gradually, Eustace took her into his confidence. Proud to have his trust, but wary of intruding, she asked no questions and patched his story together for herself from the fragments he shared.

He was born in Georgetown, British Guiana, which was in America but not the United States. Matilda thought she recognised the name from her school days, among the swathes of Empire pink that sketched a sunrise across the map on the classroom wall.

Aged fourteen, along with a brother two years his senior, Eustace stowed away on a ship bringing rum and molasses to England, arriving in Liverpool shortly ahead of the Great War.

When the brother turned eighteen, neither hesitated to serve the Mother Country, Eustace lying about his age so they could join up together. In the glittering ballroom, as the band played "Two Sleepy People", Eustace did not dwell on the horrors of the trenches. He spoke mechanically when he told Matilda he had buried his brother's body in France.

Eustace insisted he sought no special treatment. As he reminded Matilda, thousands made a bigger sacrifice. That didn't excuse the injustice meted out when the war was over. When no Black man could get a job.

Although preferring to stay in England with his brothers in arms, he would have returned to Georgetown if he could fund his passage. But he could barely afford to eat. Matilda had known poverty in early childhood, but she had not been hounded for the shade of her skin. Eustace was a few short months out of uniform when hooligans descended on the Black community in the docklands. He was forced to seek refuge in the bridewell, fearing for his life. "It weren' only Liverpool it happened. And it weren' only men they attacked." Rioting erupted in British seaports up and down the country: single men and families with children beaten and driven from their homes, their belongings stolen, their windows smashed and bonfires built from their furniture.

Eustace swanned smoothly through the dance steps as he related this ordeal, never faltering or losing his rhythm. But Matilda would have stumbled had he not held her tightly. She never saw a Negro in her coastal birthplace. Never expected to. Why was that? She hoped her neighbours had not scared them off.

Matilda's mind was spiralling between Liverpool's cobbled alleyways and the battlefields of Flanders when the band ceased playing and a whistle shrilled midway through that evening's second dance. She did not register the hand that grabbed her by the shoulder and knocked her to the floor as the matron's. The blow might have been from a shell exploding in the trenches. A thug chasing her down the street.

"Your dancing days are over, Miss." The matron hauled Matilda from the ballroom, down the corridor and up the stairs to the ward. Matilda did not see whether Eustace was banished too.

She could have fought the older woman off, but she did not dare risk further punishment. "Why? What have I done wrong?" She could still use her tongue.

"You've already brung one chance child into the world." The matron's spittle sprinkled Matilda's face. "It wouldn't be very clever if you produced a Black bastard next."

Irregular footsteps – a slide followed by a thump – stirred Matilda from her slumber in the dayroom. She opened her eyes to see her enemy haring towards her. Did the woman habitually target the seat someone else had chosen or had Matilda become complacent and inadvertently taken the bully's favourite chair? She had less than a minute to decide whether to surrender or resist.

Be kind! A Christian would turn the other cheek. Her mother's voice, as clear as if telephoning from The Willows. And as welcome. She had to act before her nemesis interpreted her grin as aggression. "Would you care to sit here?"

The woman stopped in her tracks and glared. "You're all right." She hobbled to a vacant seat nearby. Matilda noted that, with one chair between them, the woman could still prod her with her crutch.

If Matilda was friendly, would her mother speak to her again? Fortunately, she had not completely lost the art of conversation. "I haven't seen you for a while," she ventured.

The woman pursed her lips, perhaps also awaiting maternal advice. "Been on Disturbed," she said, eventually. Disturbed sounded ghastly, but the woman spoke as warmly as Matilda might mention a visit to Briarwood. If only!

"Is it frightfully grim?" asked Matilda.

"Better than here any day," said the woman. "You get wet packs."

"Wet packs?" Shopping bags for rainy weather? An underwater version of Pass the Parcel? Matilda could not fathom it.

"Never had the pleasure, posh girl?" The woman coughed and cackled with laughter. "Keep picking fights and you'll find out soon enough."

"I'm sorry if –"

"Forget it." The woman straightened her shoulders. "It weren't *you* sent me to Disturbed." She pushed back her sleeve and presented her forearm, a tapestry of scabs and scars.

"Who did that to you?" Matilda needed to know whom to avoid.

"Nobody. I done them myself." The woman withdrew her arm.

Was she lying to protect the culprit? Matilda could not envisage her *deliberately* hurting herself. Besides, how would she do it? The knives in the refectory could barely cut the slim slice of Sunday roast. The pins on her frock would not go deeper than a graze. Rather than antagonise the woman, Matilda changed the subject. "I ought to have introduced myself earlier. I'm Matilda."

The woman nodded, but did not volunteer anything of herself.

"What's your name?" In her previous life, Matilda would not have been so blunt.

"I haven't got a name no more."

Matilda bit back the responses that came to mind most readily. That she was talking nonsense. That even Ghyllside would not strip her of her name.

A flash of shame brought a memory from early childhood. She could not have been more than four or five when her mother caught her throwing stones at the beggar woman who lived in a shack at the edge of the neighbourhood. The local children said she was a witch because she talked to the rain and the gulls in the harbour and wore a stinking stole around her shoulders with a rabbit's head and floppy ears still intact. When Matilda's mother dragged her home and demanded an explanation, she knew she could not blame the older children for her cruelty. Her mother did not have to tell her she had persecuted a creature whose only crime was eccentricity; Matilda understood she had misbehaved.

Now she looked at her enemy, the madwoman, the bully, the lunatic, the cripple and recognised she too was human. Enveloped in her own misfortune, it had hardly occurred to her that others suffered too. She construed the chorus of moans in the dormitory as *her* inconvenience, not *their* distress. The only person she had tried to befriend was the foreigner, because aligning with his obvious difference helped *her* distance herself from the rest. Together they could be separate, misfits, strangers in an alien land where they had no desire to assimilate.

Perhaps a few short years older than Matilda herself, the nameless woman might have been pretty if not for her scowl and broken nose: another girl exiled from a life that had barely begun. Matilda felt a rush of pity for them both. "How did you lose it? Your name, I mean."

"My man knocked it out of me. The night he killed my babby."

"I'm sorry." Hearing her words' inadequacy, Matilda wanted to scrub them out.

"Why? You never did nowt. And *he'll* rot in jail. Though he should've hanged for it."

Would enquiring further upset her? At least *her* daughter – and her brother – were still alive. Best not to pry. But perhaps she could help the woman recover part of herself. "What was your name before that?"

"Doris."

"Doris? May I call you that?"

When she did not answer, Matilda took her shrug for *yes*.

While Matilda had stopped seeing Doris as an enemy, she still considered her too rough and unpredictable to be a friend. So when the woman hobbled towards her one Saturday afternoon as she rested in the dayroom after her work in the bakery was over, Matilda kept a watchful eye on her crutch.

Plonking herself on the adjoining chair, Doris laid her stick safely on the other side. "Sambo's been asking after you."

Matilda's stomach knotted with disparate threads of emotion, but only irritation reached her throat. "Don't call him that. His name's Eustace and he's a Zulu prince."

"Aye, and I'm Princess Lizzie of Buckingham Palace."

The conversation slain, Doris cleaned her fingernails with the pin from one of the tawdry brooches that accessorised her frock. Why did the nurses let her keep them when they had left Matilda neither handkerchief nor prayer book? Matilda hated to think of her polka-dot dress damaged by clusters of punctured fabric that would stretch to gaping holes, her favourite frock fit only for dusters and rags. But what did it matter when, barred from the ballroom, Matilda herself would have no opportunity to wear it again? Doris might as well get some satisfaction from it. And even if her leg prevented her from becoming his partner, Doris in Matilda's dress connected her to Eustace. "So what did he say?"

"That he hoped you were in good fettle and to pass on his regards."

"Anything else?"

"What were you expecting? An invitation to a tiger hunt?"

"There aren't any tigers in Africa. They live in India." Or so she believed. The longer Matilda spent in Ghyllside, the less confident she was in her knowledge of the outside world.

"Maybe he'll get to meet one."

"On the hospital farm? Hasn't he got his hands full with the pigs?"

"Not here, you barmpot. When he's discharged."

"Right." Matilda closed her eyes. Was this Doris's fantasy or Eustace's? She could not recall him expressing any interest in working in a zoo. But he was entitled to dream: a picture of heaven could cool the fires of hell.

A pinprick on her hand forced Matilda's eyes open. "Ouch." She yanked her hand away to examine it for blood, but could not detect where Doris had jabbed her. Nevertheless, invisibility did not cancel the offence.

"It's not a delusion," said Doris.

"An hallucination, then?" How ghastly to suffer visions of a tiger attack.

"You did know he might be leaving?"

"Eustace? You're having me on."

"Cross my heart and hope to die." Doris traced an X over her chest with a grubby forefinger. "Maybe he never said nowt to you about it in case you were upset."

"I'm upset he did not mention the possibility." Matilda's voice quavered. "But it's wonderful news. If it's true."

"God's gospel. There's a few of them what were soldiers likely to go. Because they'll need them, won't they, if there's another war with Germany."

"Another war?" Matilda remembered the jubilation last September when the prime minister returned from Munich with peace guaranteed.

"That's the crack from the men's side."

"But I don't understand. If Eustace is fit to fight for his country, why was he in Ghyllside in the first place? And if he's mental, why send him to war? He wouldn't have a chance."

"Don't ask me," said Doris. "I'm not a doctor. Anyroad, if it gets him out of here, who cares?"

"I care."

"You could get a gun and join up too." Like a boy playing cowboys, Doris made a pistol of her fingers and mimed taking shots at the surrounding chairs.

As a tear rolled down her cheek, Matilda registered its temperature and its progress, but she could not tell whether she cried for Eustace or for herself.

"You weren't sweet on him, were you?" said Doris. "I mean, not in *that* way."

"Of course not. It's ... my brother."

"Your brother? Is he handsome? Scared a Nazi's bayonet's gonna ruin his looks?"

Matilda laughed through her tears. "He's only six. It'll be a few more years before he gets called up."

"Well then."

"I never got to say a proper goodbye to him," Matilda sobbed. "He'll think I vanished into thin air." She clicked her fingers. "Like that."

"Can he read?"

"Of course he can. But the doctor has forbidden me to write to him. Says it's better he forgets."

"Evil berk," said Doris. "Is there a telephone at Osborne Mansions?"

"What use is that if I can't get past Sister? She's like a Bengal tiger guarding the crown jewels."

"I'll see to it."

"If only you could."

"Didn't I tell you? The nurses don't run this ward. I do."

Doris did not reveal her plan to enable Matilda to access the ward telephone, but she did arrange for her to send a farewell note to Eustace despite being denied both writing paper and ink. Matilda did not relish Doris rousing her from sleep and ushering her to the lavatories the moment a particularly lackadaisical night nurse put her feet up in the office and began to snore.

Summer's heat intensified the stench and the moonlight exposed the smears of menstrual blood and faecal matter on walls, porcelain and tile. It was not a place to linger, as the responsibility for cleaning the area fell to patients who were too disturbed and incapable to work in the bakery, laundry or kitchens, and who could not be trusted with bleach. When Doris gave Matilda a few sheets of medicated paper, stamped GOVERNMENT PROPERTY, and pointed her towards the windowsill, Matilda dampened it at the basin and used it – as far as possible, given its poor absorbency – to swab the ledge.

Doris tutted. "We seem to be out of parchment, madam. You'll have to make do with bog roll." She handed her a few more sheets of Izal and a pin.

Suddenly self-conscious, Matilda hunched over the paper, like a schoolgirl in an exam. Its smell, although unpleasant, partly neutralised the odour in the air. Unfortunately, whether she tried scratching the rough side or the smooth side, it was hopeless: the pin either tore the paper or left no mark.

"You'll be popular the morrow when they've nowt to wipe their bums with." Doris snatched the pin and pierced Matilda's thumb, releasing a tiny red bauble from her skin. "Was you never blood-sisters in them posh houses? Now, get writing! Nurse Ninny won't keep her eyes shut for ever and I want my bed."

Matilda had pondered the wording several times a day since Doris first mooted the idea. She wanted something cordial but not overfamiliar, something that would disgrace neither of them if her note were discovered. A line of verse would have done the job but, at this hour, attempting to recall the poetry she had learnt by rote – at school or with her mother for public-speaking contests – was like trying to catch a bubble or a dandelion clock.

She need not have bothered. Doris's strategy, although better than nothing, made even a short message a challenge. GOOD LUCK YOUR FRIEND MATILDA would have to suffice.

Tiptoeing back to the dormitory, while relieved to have escaped the night nurse's attention, Matilda felt a hollowness which was not solely from the paltry diet. Doubtful, despite Doris's promise, she could contact Henry by telephone, Matilda had wondered if she might ask Eustace to smuggle a letter out.

But no language, however lyrical, could cushion the shock of a missive scrawled on toilet paper in his sister's blood.

Chapter 8: June, 1964

After stepping off the bus, they tail the passengers streaming away from the gloom and the stench of petrol into the light. Dazzled by the sun, Matty almost collides with a mother pushing a pram. Time peels back and she searches for Henry swaddled inside it. Time zips forward to reveal not a *lady* steering the baby past the bus station, but a *man*. A man pushing a pram!

Her brain is a boxing ring where novelty jostles with memory. How can she recognise what is real? She is a schoolgirl again, baffled by Greek and Latin, afraid of being left behind.

With scant regard for Doris's limp, Matty runs, veering left and sprinting past Windsor's Haberdashery. A car horn beeps as she dashes across the road. Halfway down the street, passing the chemist Timothy White's with the Ritz picture palace opposite, a stabbing pain in her side brings her to her senses. She stops to recover her breath and for Doris to catch up.

"What was that in aid of?" says Doris. "Spot somebody you owe money to?"

She could say she wanted to buy aspirin. Whisper she needed a sanitary towel. Gazing through the window for inspiration,

Matty perceives not shelves of shampoo, soap and medicine bottles but tables with red banquette seating. Somehow she has drifted from the pharmacy to a restaurant. Matty cannot remember what style of shop occupied this space twenty-five years ago.

"You must be famished, missing breakfast," says Doris.

In response, Matty's stomach gurgles. Although not yet ready to speak, Doris's thoughtfulness anchors her. Restores her to herself.

Meanwhile, Doris has turned her attention to the menu plastered to the window. Like a baby's first book, it favours pictures over words. Ignoring the plated meals – heaps of slim chipped potatoes accompanying thick chops or squares of breaded fish – she points to the rissoles cushioned between white buns. "If we go for them butties, you'll still have change from ten bob."

"Hamburgers," Matty reads aloud. The colours in the photographs must be distorted, as the minced meat is not pink enough for ham. "German, by the name."

"Give over," says Doris. "You'd choke on Nazi food."

She may not have heard of Hamburg, says Matty's mother.

The Wimpy Bar appears more inviting than the dining room on Ward 24. There is a choice of unoccupied tables and sufficient female diners to reassure her that this bar's climate would have nothing in common with a pub, not that Matty has ever been inside one. Without tablecloths, it seems less ostentatious than the hotel restaurant in the Lake District where they once celebrated her mother's birthday. More modern. And now the Nazis have been annihilated, it should be safe, morally and medically, to sample German cuisine. Nevertheless, after battling Ghyllside's revolving doors, she may no longer have the oomph to cross another threshold. "We could buy picnic food from Marks and Spencer. Bread rolls, tomatoes and cheese." They could go to Mill Field, if Doris can walk that far. If they can find some shade.

"I'm easy," says Doris. "It's your dosh."

It is not the money that makes Matty dither. She would happily treat her friend. But would they be welcome? Would her mother approve?

The door opens and a man in a chef's white coat and tall hat pops his head through the gap. "Are you lunching, ladies? If you come in now, before it gets busy, I can give you a soft drink on the house." The decision is made.

Following him inside to a table, Doris grins. For Matty, it is not so much his offer of a free glass of squash that attracts her, but his respect. It is as if, despite the cash in her purse, she expected to be received like a beggar. Here, they are not patients but valued customers.

They each pluck a cardboard menu from the silvery metal holder, something to study until they are brave enough to survey their wider surroundings. At the hotel, the menu came in a book bound in leather with a separate folder for the wine. As a girl of twelve, Matty's sentiments swung between sophisticated and intimidated, but the account she shared with her schoolmates emphasised the glamour.

Doris sets her menu aside to pick up what appears to be a child's plastic toy, the shape and hue of a giant tomato. Both women gasp when, squeezing too hard, blood-coloured sauce shoots onto Doris's chin. When no one else notices, their eyes meet and they giggle, albeit quietly. This meal promises to be fun.

Before Matty can retrieve her hanky from her sleeve, Doris has cleansed her chin with a paper serviette. Stamped with the restaurant's name and a cartoon chef, it is almost too good to use. But, having used it, Doris does not let it go to waste. She hides the stain in its folds and stuffs it in her waistcoat pocket.

A smiling girl brings their drinks and jots down their order. Matty imagines wearing that waitress uniform herself one day: a black dress with an oversized white collar topped with an apron to match the crimson seats. The girl's auburn hair is crowned with a dainty cap not dissimilar to the one the nurses wear at Ghyllside except that the Wimpy's version is red.

The waitress saunters to the back of the restaurant, where she reaches across a chrome counter to pass the chit to the chef. *How irregular*, remarks Matty's mother. *They have dispensed with a separate kitchenette*.

Although she always bows to her mother's grace and wisdom, Matty finds the openness refreshing. She can watch their food being cooked. She can smell the onions browning and, above the murmur of conversation, imagine hearing the meat sizzling as it cooks. The ambience is so honest that Matty relaxes enough to remove her handbag from her lap and place it between her feet on the chessboard-tiled floor.

Their hamburgers arrive promptly, extravagantly presented with a serviette between bun and plate, although the waitress neglects to deliver the cutlery. Matty blushes when Doris lifts the lid of her bun to squirt tomato sauce on the fried onions and picks it up to eat it, like an ordinary sandwich, with her hands. But, seeing the men on the neighbouring table tuck in in similar fashion, Matty follows suit.

They chew without speaking, savouring the textures and tastes. The bread is softer and spongier than Ghyllside's bakery ever produced. The onions melt on the tongue. Although the meat could come from any animal, it is richer and more tender than Ghyllside's Sunday roast.

Finished, Doris wipes her fingers on the serviette. "So, what now? Are you gonna show me the sights?"

The sights! says her mother. *Has she mistaken the town for Blackpool or Bowness?*

Matty could spend a wistful afternoon visiting the landmarks of her youth: the Carnegie library; the Stanley Hall ballroom; St Mark's church with her mother's grave. But Doris, although supportive, is the wrong companion for such a pilgrimage and she lacks the courage to wander alone. "We mustn't be late for the circus."

Doris exhumes the poster from her pocket and smooths it out on the table between them. The first performance is at three. "Bags of time."

As the waitress approaches, Matty gestures at the corners of her mouth and dabs them with a serviette, hoping Doris will interpret her face as a mirror and clear the ketchup from her own. Doris does not take the hint.

The waitress collects their plates. "Can I get you anything else, ladies? Coffee? Dessert?"

Matty fancies a slice of the apple pie she noticed on the menu card earlier but they must not overspend. A hot drink would be more affordable. "Do you have Ovaltine or Horlicks?" At Ghyllside there is only cocoa and tea.

"Let's have coffee," Doris interjects, before the waitress can reply.

Has she ever tried coffee? Matty's mother asks.

The waitress glances from Doris to Matty. "Two coffees?"

It is a day for new experiences. A day to be reborn as modern women. Matty nods.

When the waitress leaves them, Doris takes a packet of Woodbines and a box of matches from her pocket. She extracts a cigarette and holds it between her lips. Before she can strike a match, a young man in an open-necked shirt and blue blazer springs from his seat, flicks his lighter and ignites her cigarette from the flame.

"Thank you." Doris exhales tobacco-scented smoke.

"My pleasure." The gentleman returns to his table.

Treated like royalty, says Matty's mother. *If Sister could see you now!*

Doris is stubbing out her cigarette in the ashtray when their coffees arrive. Matty's requires four sugar lumps to neutralise the bitterness. Doris's needs five. Yet the fragrance is delicious, as is their sense of themselves as they sip.

"Clara doesn't know what she's missing," says Doris.

They have almost finished when the man in the blue blazer advances towards their table. "Sorry to interrupt, ladies." Although his accent is coarse, his manner is chivalrous. "I see you've got the poster for Billy Smart's at The Cloffocks. Mind if I have a decko?"

Doris slides it across the table. After a cursory squint, he calls over his shoulder to his friend. "It's ages yet." With a heartfelt "Thank you", he steps away. Then seems to reconsider. "If you've got time to kill before the show, would you let a pair of ugly lads buy you lasses a drink?"

His friend sniggers, Matty assumes because the men are far from ugly, although both have thick locks almost reaching their collars, long overdue a trim. The man still seated wears a tan blazer that matches his hair and freckles.

"We are respectable ladies," says Doris, struggling not to smile.

"I don't doubt it," says the man. "But you've nowt to fear from us. We're in the business of citizen protection." He cocks his head in the direction of the freckled fellow, who shields the lower half of his face with his hand. "Neville's a fireman and I'm with the police."

"That's good to know," says Doris. "This is the Honourable Matilda, a distant cousin of Queen Elizabeth, although we don't stand on ceremony. You can address her as Matty."

The man bows. "So, what's it to be, Matty?"

Doris widens her eyes but, as a mere lady-in-waiting, *she* can neither accept nor refuse the invitation. Matty listens for advice from her mother, but she has faded out of range. She drains her coffee cup, but her mouth remains dry. "We could accept a second glass of orange squash."

"Here?" The man glances about him, his brow furrowed. "I mean, it's all right, but we could take you somewhere with a bit more atmosphere."

Matty has an uncomfortable feeling he has in mind a pub. But she is helpless against the pressure of Doris's desire. And joining the men would excuse her from showing Doris the sights.

Chapter 9: October, 1939

My darling brother,

I am so sorry I missed your birthday and that my homecoming has once more been delayed. But the war having turned so many lives inside out, who am I to grumble?

I know you must miss me – as I miss you – but I hope you are proud that I am playing my part in the fight against Hitler, albeit at a safe distance from the front. Can you imagine, I am now an orderly in a military hospital? Although the work is tiring, the patients are real gentlemen, and we girls have fun.

They say this war will be over by Christmas and I look forward to helping you hang up your stocking and cooking an enormous dinner. Until then, be a brave little soldier for me, and remember me in your prayers.

Your loving sister,
Tilly.

———

Doris's limp seemed less severe as she crossed the airing court. Yet she had not abandoned her crutch. Glad to be outside, while alert for signs of impending violence, Matilda envied her friend her deterrent. In seven months' incarceration, she had observed that even the most docile of the detainees would lash out occasionally, particularly if they were agitated or provoked. Although Matilda herself relished the glimpse of sky above the asylum buildings, the fenced enclosure made others nervous. One old woman saw spectres in the wind.

But the day was calm, albeit cool and cloudy, as Doris fell into jerky step beside her. "Get ready to speak to your brother. Nurse Ninny's on days."

Matilda glanced to where the nurse stood smoking in the door frame of the rear staircase to Ward 24. Nurse Ninny had a proper name, although Matilda did not know it. She knew her weakness, however, which both excited and scared her. Patients had more freedom when Nurse Ninny was on duty – freedom which had allowed a diagnosed moral degenerate to dance with a man from a different race – but would she have the gumption to get them to safety in the event of a fire? "I doubt she would let me use the telephone. Not even for a bottle of rum." And, as far as she was aware, Doris had not established a distillery in Ghyllside's kitchens, or anywhere else on the site.

"You're learning, posh girl. Maybe you *won't* collapse when I leave."

Doris getting her discharge? That is as credible as Germany winning the war. Matilda froze at the sound of mother. It was happening more and more, mostly at night but sometimes, when she was particularly fatigued, in the daytime. After the initial shock, she found it a comfort, but dreaded the nurses finding out. They seemed to delight in stripping the inmates of whatever helped them bear their trials.

Doris gripped her arm and hurried her along. They weren't compelled to use the airing court for exercise but, coatless in the autumn chill, walking the boundary – a mere minute's leisurely perambulation – made more sense than standing still.

"Anyroad," Doris continued, "I've got stronger weapons than bribery to beat the bastards. Effing Nazis."

"I hope you won't get into trouble on my account." Doris had taken a risk already with that letter.

"They can't pain me more than me husband done."

Matilda shuddered. Doris had lost everything but her enamel badges and a willingness to fight. "Is there a plan?"

"Best you don't know the details. You might cock it up. But, when I give the signal, you call her out of the office and grab the phone."

Just like that? Doris made it sound like a spy story, or a game. Yet, Matilda reminded herself, although her methods were crude, Doris got results. She had delivered her message to Eustace. And brought one back, transcribed not in blood but in the ruddy petals of a rose. That summer, Matilda envied the men permitted to work outside.

She would have loved to keep the flower. But where would she get a vase or even a cup to fill with water? Where would she get a weighty book to press the bloom between its pages? Yet, marching to church on Sunday mornings, her spirits lifted at the sight of the rose beds. Testament to her resistance and rebellion. And his.

Now Doris proposed a graver transgression than accepting a token of friendship from her dancing partner, with detection and punishment virtually guaranteed. But Matilda would pay any price to hear her brother. To reassure him she cared. "What signal?"

"You'll know when you see it."

Before she could ask for clarification, a whistle summoned the patients to the door. Nurse Ninny stepped aside as they clumped up the stairs, Doris and her gammy leg lagging behind. The nurse was last, locking the door behind her. Matilda's stomach curdled with a muddle of anticipation and dread.

Returned to the ward, the patients settled into the armchairs. The nurse went directly to the office and closed the door. She showed so little concern for her charges, Matilda thought she would have drawn a curtain across the observation window had there been one.

Doris coughed into her fist. Matilda sidled up to her. "Was that the signal?" Doris's secrecy doubled Matilda's anxiety: not only might she fail to persuade her father to let her speak to her brother but she might miss Doris's cue.

"You're keen. I never reckoned on doing it today. But if you want ..." Doris became positively perky.

What *did* Matilda want? She wanted the escapade to be over. She wanted longer to prepare. But, guessing the hour from the ward routine, she knew the time was ripe. "Henry will be home from school." Hopefully with an amenable girl for company. "His father will be at work."

"Let me get my props." As Doris shambled off towards the lavatories, Matilda made to follow. Doris shooed her away. "Sit down, you berk. Don't let on you're waiting for me."

Matilda found her mind as wobbly as her legs as she attempted to compose herself. How should she approach the call? Naturally, her brother would not answer the telephone. Matilda would have to convince the girl. She would introduce herself as the mother of one of his school friends ringing to … To invite him to a birthday party, of course. Once he heard her voice, Henry would forgive the deception. A moment with the sister who had cherished him from infancy would mean more to him than cake, Pass the Parcel and Musical Bumps.

She was beginning to believe in the story, when Doris stumbled into the dayroom. Matilda did not need to feign consternation at the sight of her friend's face and arms streaked with blood. This surpassed her expectations. Doris could not have done this with a pin.

Bolting from her seat, Matilda dashed towards the casualty. Grimacing, Doris flapped her away. Seconds later, Matilda hammered on the pane of glass in the office door. "Nurse! Nurse! She's gone demented." Nurse Ninny languidly stubbed out a cigarette.

How could she be so complacent? Matilda rapped until her knuckles stung. Frantic, she turned back towards the dayroom. If Nurse Ninny ignored Doris's lacerations, Matilda would have to rip up her frock and bandage them herself.

Doris paraded her injuries in front of the observation window, a crazed grin contorting her face. She seemed to taunt Nurse Ninny when she banged on the window, tucked her crutch under her armpit and started to split the skin of her forearm with a shard of glass. The woman was mad.

The nurse almost knocked Matilda over as she rocketed out of the office. Matilda fixed her mind on Henry as she launched herself inside. Her hand shook as she lifted the receiver of the Bakelite telephone and dialled the three digits. Her mouth dried as she waited. She rested her buttocks on the edge of the desk, her back to the observation window to avoid being distracted by the butchery outside. She must not squander this opportunity.

When a lady responded with a request for the number instead of *Good afternoon, this is The Willows, how may I help?* Matilda dithered, wasting precious moments before she realised the hospital must use a switchboard. Luckily, the operator did not challenge her right to make a call.

When the connection was made, a gentleman answered. Although surprised, wondering if, in her panic, she had given the telephonist the wrong number, Matilda screwed up her eyes and kept to her script. In the role of a schoolboy's mother, she asked if she might have a word with young Henry. "It will only take a minute." Matilda could not rely on Doris's charade granting her even that.

Her appeal was met with heavy breathing, as if an elderly man were collecting his thoughts. But neither she nor Henry had known their grandparents.

Then came words fit to burst her eardrum. "You *must* be tapped Matilda, if you think I'd fall for that pantomime."

Her eyes snapped open, but all she saw was the dusty blackboard nailed to the opposite wall. Had Doris harmed herself for nothing? "Please, Father, let me speak to him. I promise I won't upset him. I'm desperate to hear his voice."

"That's impossible."

"If not for my sake, for his. He must miss me. Let me explain I can't come back."

"You've always had an inflated sense of your own importance. He's happy without you. Besides, he isn't here."

Not at home? At a real party? "May I ring another day?" She had to ask, although the chance might never arise.

"My son is at boarding school."

"Boarding school? He's only six." How could a father be so cruel? The boy would be bereft without a bedtime story. Without someone who loved him to hear his prayers.

"Seven. It was his birthday last week."

"Oh." Blowing out his candles among strangers. Unwrapping his presents alone. If such frivolities were permitted at boarding school. His deprivation exacerbated by her absence, in spirit as well as in body. What had Ghyllside done to her that she had not marked the date? But she could make it up to him. "He'll be home for Christmas?"

"That's no business of yours. So don't think you can bother him in the holidays. I'll have your guts for garters if you try to get in touch again. Henry doesn't *have* a sister. You're of no consequence to him."

The receiver fell from her hand. Matilda almost fell with it. She could have dropped through the floor, crashed through the ceiling of the ward below and continued sinking through the earth. There was nothing to hold her.

Except Doris. Matilda straightened. She grabbed the ceramic ashtray from the desk and flung it at the blackboard. When that produced a healthy crack, she snatched Nurse Ninny's china cup and saucer and hurled them after it.

Subjected to the cold wet pack treatment, Matilda hoped never to repeat the experience. Doris claimed it calmed her to be trussed in wet sheets like a swaddled baby but, bound so tightly her body could barely shiver, Matilda thought it more akin to an Egyptian mummy being prepared for burial. If Doris had not been lying on the bed beside hers, she would have lost her mind.

Fortunately, they could turn their heads to see each other. When the nurses left, they could talk, although Matilda felt as constrained by what she could say as by her shroud. Doubting that Doris would tell her how she had hidden that spike of glass, she asked about her wounds. "Does it hurt much?"

"Tingles."

"Why did you do it?" Matilda could not complain. Doris had sacrificed more than she had. Although the bleeding had stopped, her face was scribbled with abrasions. Beneath her bindings, her arms and legs were in shreds.

"Cause it were criminal leaving that little lad in the dark. It were worth a couple of scratches to let him know you weren't dead. What did you tell him?"

"Tell him?"

"About why you couldn't come home."

Matilda could have pretended the conversation was confidential, but Doris did not deserve to be brushed off. Nor should she share the burden of defeat. The failure was Matilda's alone. "I said I was working for the war office." Matilda lightened her tone. "Top-secret mission. Very hush-hush."

"Brilliant. He'll be proud but he'll know not to brag about it. Careless talk costs lives."

"I said I was safe in a bunker. So he wouldn't worry about Hitler's bombs."

"Could happen."

"This place feels more like a mausoleum."

"Maybe not for much longer. Maybe the war will set us free."

A girl at the nunnery had thought likewise, back when Matilda had hope. "If Eustace can get his discharge, why not us?" Matilda did not believe the war would save her, but she owed Doris her gratitude and words were all she had to give.

Chapter 10: June, 1964

When they head off in the direction of the railway station, Matty wonders if they'll go as far as the dockland area where she lived until the age of twelve. There is a pub on every street at that end of town. Or was, when she and her friends inhaled the inns' beery breath on passing their open doors. Walking alongside Neville, the freckly fireman, she looks back intermittently, remembering Doris's suggestion she show her the sights. But, either due to her limp or Aidan monopolising her attention, Doris lags behind.

"All right, Matty?" asks Neville.

"Yes, thank you." But Matty is not all right. Aidan's invitation did not mention dividing into couples. It would be perfectly acceptable if they planned to go dancing, but she and Doris would be on the bus back to Ghyllside before the band warmed up. It would be tolerable if they were better balanced, but she and Neville have barely exchanged a dozen words, whereas Doris and Aidan chinwag like brother and sister reunited after decades apart. It is a blessed relief when Neville leads her into a saloon bar a short distance down a side street. Matty feels more reassured when Doris and Aidan join them at a highly-polished table, and Neville gets up to fetch drinks from the bar.

"This is more fun than a smelly old circus," says Doris.

Matty frowns. "We're still going, aren't we?"

"We won't stop you," says Aidan. "If that's what you want."

"But you might feel different after a few bevvies." Neville unloads two pint glasses and two half-pint tankards onto the table from a gaily-painted metal tray. Brown ale capped with froth for the men and amber fizz for the ladies. Taking a tentative sip of what she assumes to be cider, Matty detects no trace of apple but, nevertheless, finds the brew refreshing.

"So, you're just here for the day, girls?" says Aidan. "Then it's back to the country pile?"

"Unless we get a better offer." Doris seems to have forgotten that a lady-in-waiting must defer to her mistress.

"What have you done with your chauffeur while you're slumming with the proles?" says Neville.

Matty swigs her cider while waiting for Doris to fathom a reply. She had not realised how thirsty she was. She swallows almost half the contents of her glass.

"Or is it a secret?" says Aidan. "Perhaps you murdered him."

"And picked us up as an alibi," says Neville.

Doris scowls. *Perhaps she remembers her murderous husband,* says Matty's mother. *Or she does not know the meaning of chauffeur.*

So it falls to Matty, ordinarily so quiet, to return the volley. "We prefer to commit our murders in the cooler months. We sent Jeeves to visit his aged mother. We'll travel back by bus." Somewhat alarmed, she picks at the corner of a cardboard beer mat with her thumbnail. Yet their collective laughter bubbles like applause.

"I'm glad you're not stuffy, Matty," says Neville. "Like some of the Cumberland gentry." Is it her imagination, or has he edged his chair closer to hers?

Neville takes out a pipe and fills the bowl with tobacco, tamping it down with his thumb. Aidan lights two cigarettes and slips one between Doris's lips. As she sucks in the smoke, Matty notices tomato sauce dotting the corners of her mouth, despite the coffee and cider that ought to have diluted it. She cannot think how to tell Doris to wipe her mouth without also alerting the men. She would hate to embarrass her friend.

"You're not a smoker, Matty?" says Aidan.

Doris extends her bottom lip and exhales towards the nicotine-stained ceiling. "It doesn't agree with her voice."

"Though good for the lungs," says Neville.

Doris leans forward. "Matty performs in music halls in her spare time."

The men's eyes widen. Matty feels equally surprised, but she would not contradict her friend. Indeed, she feels uplifted. Forget waitressing, she might make the stage her future career. *A natural progression,* says her mother. *Remember the rosettes you won for public speaking as a child.*

"What's your line, Matty?" says Neville. "Can-can dancing? Burlesque?"

"I recite comic verse."

"Let me get another round in," says Aidan, rising from his seat. "Then you can give us a taster. If you don't mind?"

"I'd be delighted."

Since they are the only patrons in the snug, when Aidan returns with the drinks, Matty gets to her feet and delivers a perfect rendition of Hilaire Belloc's "Matilda Who Told Lies and Was Burned to Death". Her monologue leaves her breathless, although it could be the rapturous applause, not only from the trio at the table but also the barman drying glasses with a towel.

As she sinks into her seat, Neville pats her on the back. "Brilliant choice for a fireman. Although I'd come out to save you any day."

"And I'd never arrest you, no matter how many lies you told," says Aidan.

The men discuss the poems they learnt at school. Matty tries to join in, but her brain is too sluggish. No doubt due to the heat.

At the tinkle of a bell, Matty looks up to see the barman replace a brass hand-bell on the counter. "Last orders!" he booms, like a town crier.

Neville gets up, but Aidan restrains him. He glances back and forth between Matty and Doris. "If you want to catch the three o'clock show, it's best to leave now. But if you're not that bothered, we can have another drink."

Matty feels torn, but Doris is resolute. She takes the poster from her pocket, screws it into a ball and tosses it into the ashtray. She strikes a match, but Neville blows it out before she can put it to the paper. Matty appreciates his caution. As Aidan said earlier in the Wimpy Bar, their business is protection.

Neville buys more drinks. Aidan invites Doris to help him choose records for the jukebox, a coin-operated gramophone that would befit a fairground. Matty sees Aidan stroke Doris's posterior. She does not see Doris shove his hand away.

Matty recognises the melody. But now, as Doris accepts a kiss from Aidan and they promenade back to the table, "I Want to Hold Your Hand" sounds sinister and somewhat lewd. Neville sets a glass of cider Matty does not want on the table in front of her. She does not want his arm around her shoulders either, but it would be rude to shake him off. She should have gone to The Cloffocks to watch the circus when she had the chance.

A woman is singing "I Just Don't Know What to Do with Myself" when the barman rings the bell again. "Time please!" A strange request when he need only tilt his head to see the clock on the wall above the shelves of wines and spirits behind him.

"Drink up!" Neville holds the glass to her lips as if she were a child.

Matty gulps down half of it to be polite, and turns away. Neville finishes it off.

The others stand. Matty sways slightly as she rises. She feels both grateful and resentful when Neville takes her arm. "We're leaving already?" It seems barely ten minutes since they decided to stay.

"Pub's closing," says Neville. "I asked for a lock-in but it's not worth his while."

Matty's heart seems to skip a beat. They would not believe that she and Doris were locked in for years. They would suffocate if trapped in the pub.

"But we won't let the licensing laws spoil our fun," says Doris. "We're going back to Aidan's for our own little party."

"I need the lavatory," whispers Matty.

"You can go at my place," says Aidan.

Matty is mortified he has overheard. But the pressure on her bladder is even more uncomfortable. "I'm desperate."

Neville urges her towards the door. "The bogs here aren't fit for a lady. You'd be better off at Aidan's. It's not far."

Chapter 11: March/April, 1940

My darling brother,

I hope you are enjoying boarding school and have lots of new chums. My best friend here is called Doris. I think you would like her. She would love to meet you.

I have been a little low lately, with the war dragging on so. Although I am sure I will rally. I just need to give myself a shake and count my blessings.

Words cannot describe how much I miss you, but God watches over us and He will reunite us soon. It should not be too long until Hitler is defeated and we can be together again. Be a brave boy in the meantime, Henry, and remember me in your prayers. As I remember you in mine.

Your loving sister,

Tilly.

ele

In the year since she had laboured in the convent, Matilda had given little thought to the reason she went there and the daughter she could not take with her when she left. For an entire year, her detachment seemed logical: not wanting to keep the baby, what was there to mourn?

Now, inured to the rhythms of the asylum, grief bubbled to the surface. What she took for indifference must have been a state of overwhelm. With the injustice of incarceration and separation from her brother, her mind could not accommodate more sorrow.

She would awaken at night to the sound of an infant calling *Ma-ma*. She would startle herself in the daytime, rocking an absence in her arms. Her breasts felt tender and bloated. Lullabies trilled in her ears.

Once or twice she was on the brink of confiding in Doris. But she hesitated to remind her friend of *her* lost child. The pain of a newborn whisked away for adoption paled to insignificance relative to seeing a child with substance and personality murdered before her eyes.

One miserable morning Matilda almost confessed to the nurse, but she had enough wit to hold back. Psychiatry construed strange sensations as madness. The law framed unmarried motherhood as depraved. But even if they were sympathetic, no one could undo the damage. Her only chance of release from this torture was to forget.

With typical perversity, the nurses summoned her to the dormitory again on Friday evenings to choose a frock for the dance. Now that her partner had departed, now that she despised joviality, they demanded Matilda make merry. Doris was more lenient, requiring no more than Matilda's physical presence. Neither wore the polka-dot dress.

For someone whose lameness made her a liability on the dancefloor, Doris had lofty ambitions for Friday nights. Unmoved by the music, immune to flirtation, she was there to tune in to the jungle telegraph. With no access to newspapers, few visitors, and staff who had neither time nor inclination for casual conversation, Ghyllside seemed designed to keep inmates in ignorance. Doris, her cunning manifest in her collection of sharp instruments concealed in the lavatory cistern, seemed designed to circumvent restrictions.

At work in the kitchens, Doris gathered scraps of gossip from the women from other wards. Maybe one had had a letter, another a visitor, yet another a snatched exchange with an orderly who did not view patients as less worthy than dogs. Alone, these crumbs might seem trivial, but combined they produced a crust that would not exist otherwise and, occasionally, a cake.

The ballroom being the only part of the asylum where the sexes could mingle, Doris prioritised quizzing the men. Her leg might ache so much that even a slow waltz was beyond her, still she would stand up to sway, clinging to her partner and pumping him for information. Whenever she gleaned some fresh intelligence, she would weave through the couples and report to Matilda, before passing it on to anyone else who cared to know.

Thus Matilda learnt that the patient population was swelling with evacuees from another asylum now requisitioned as a military hospital. She learnt that Nurse Ninny had been transferred to the gruesome Incontinent Ward where the conchies served their time. She learnt of the doctors' plan to interview every patient to assess their suitability for discharge.

"I told you our turn would come," said Doris.

A year ago, she dreamt of joining the Women's Royal Navy if she could find her sea legs; now, she could not take a bath alone. She dreamt of new horizons, yet her life had stalled before it had properly begun. New dreams entailed new disappointments. If only she could erase this life, like a timeworn lesson from the blackboard, and begin again.

"Not us," said Matilda. "They only want the men."

"If we let you out, would you go after your brother?"

"Of course. He is everything to me." Matilda's spine stiffened with renewed resolve.

"No!" Doris's crutch smacked the chair leg, narrowly missing Matilda's foot. "Are you crazy?"

"It's the truth. I will contact every school in the country until I find him. I will not give up."

According to Doris's sources, the doctors had trawled the male side for potential discharges. It would not be long before they checked the female wards. Determined they should both be ready for their interview, Doris insisted they rehearse their responses to ensure the right result. "Truth's no good to nobody if it keeps you locked up. You've got to tell them what they want to hear. So, repeat after me, *I want what's best for Henry. And that means never seeing him no more.*"

"I want what's best for Henry. That means never seeing him again."

"Nearly," said Doris. "Have another bash, but without that crack in your voice halfway through."

"I cannot lie." Even if she could settle it with her conscience, she would not be brazen enough to convince the doctors.

"Not even to save your skin?"

"They probably won't ask me about him." What was she saying? It was as if she believed they would include her. As if she had succumbed to hope.

"After you forced your friend to create a diversion so you could dart into the office and use the telephone? They'll ask you all right."

Matilda had not construed claiming to be the mother of Henry's school mate as lying, merely playing a part.

As a child, she often recited a poem about a girl called Matilda whose lies had disastrous consequences. Part cautionary tale, part amusing bagatelle, she had loved and feared it in equal measure. Could she temporarily adopt the role of the lying Matilda and switch back to herself once she was free? She cocked her head, hoping to pick up her mother's opinion on the matter but, if she had any advice to offer, it was lost in the jangled orchestra of hooting and cawing from the wretches at the other end of the room. No doctor would consider *them* for discharge. But Matilda's case had nothing in common with theirs.

"Remember your Zulu prince?" said Doris.

"Eustace? He wasn't a prince and of course I remember him. I'm not gaga."

"You were fond of him, weren't you?"

"He was a gentleman."

"And a killer."

Matilda had almost risen from her seat, prepared to punch the other woman, when she saw a nurse leave the office and glance towards them. She couldn't bear to be sent back to Disturbed. "That's slander," she hissed.

"Not really," said Doris. "I'll admit I can't prove he *personally* killed someone. But every man who signed up to fight had to be prepared to have blood on his hands. And there's you bothered about staining your soul with a tiddly white lie."

"That's different."

"Is it?" said Doris.

"Fletcher!" screeched the nurse.

Matilda would not have realised she was addressing Doris until her friend began scrabbling on the floor for her crutch. It had been difficult enough to discover her Christian name; she had not envisaged her having a surname too.

Doris rose from her seat as the nurse approached. Matilda could not understand why she seemed so eager when the nurse wore the standard grim expression.

"Wash your face and run a comb through your hair," said the nurse. "The doctor wants to see you."

Matilda's head felt as light as a balloon. Her vision blurred. Was this really happening? Would they actually have the chance to leave? She was so astonished she did not manage to wish Doris good luck as she hobbled away.

She recovered in time to race after the nurse and catch her before she reached the office. "Excuse me, Miss. Will the doctor see me too?"

~elle~

Sleet lashed the darkening windows of the dayroom. A patient snored. Most of the others were in the dormitory, choosing their glad rags for the dance. Only Matilda and Doris, and a few waifs who could not distinguish their toes from their elbows, let alone use them to foxtrot or waltz, remained in the lounge.

Matilda tried to smooth the rough fabric of her frock. "Are you sure you don't want to go, Doris? It might cheer you up."

"You go, I'm not stopping you."

"I'd rather keep you company."

"I don't need mollycoddling. There's nowt wrong."

Matilda thought her grimace implied the opposite. Like a sulky child. "You've barely said a word to me all week."

"There's nowt to say."

"Nothing to say?" Matilda wanted to shake her. "You get a job – a real job out in the world – and you have nothing to say about it? No news to share with your friend left behind?"

"I'm tired."

Matilda's eyes stung. How thrilled she had felt when Doris emerged from her interview with the doctor. How hopeful that the trial period in the munitions factory would become permanent and her friend would be discharged. With her mother's encouragement, she had tamped down her envy to prevent it diminishing Doris's delight. How dare she dismiss her so carelessly? "Tired? You should try being hauled out of bed before five every morning. You should try begging the nurses for ten minutes with the doctor and being constantly rebuffed."

As Doris smouldered, Matilda stayed vigilant, ready to jump from her seat if Doris reached for her crutch. But Doris's hands remained in her lap. "Want to know why I'm tired? Want to know what it's like?" She would not have been able to grasp her stick even if she wanted to, she was trembling so much. "An hour on the bus out to Drigg of a morning. An hour on the bus coming back. Too late to eat with the rest of you, and if you think that slop's disgusting hot, you should try eating it cold. A long shift in between, boring as hell, just like here, except that laundry soap isn't explosive and Hitler's not gonna bomb a loony bin."

Matilda extended her hand to pat her shoulder, noticed her scowl, and withdrew. "But the other girls? They must be interesting? They must know more about what's going on?"

Doris sniffed. "Never met such a snooty lot in my life. And they've no excuse for their airs and graces. None of them talk proper like you."

"There must be someone decent among them." Matilda laughed, unclear whether she was pleased or disappointed Doris hadn't yet made a friend.

"If there is, she hides it well. They won't even let us from Ghyllside share their table in the canteen. Scared they'll catch summat off us."

A patient drifted into the dayroom and made a swift retreat. She was dressed for the dance but Matilda could not discern whether her red frock had white spots.

"The first week is bound to be the worst." Matilda tried to sound convincing but even she doubted her words. She had adapted to the rhythms of the hospital but, in some ways, it seemed harder as the months went by and hope faded. Yet this was different. "You mustn't let it beat you. I'm sure they'll accept you once you're discharged."

"No skin off my nose if they don't," said Doris. "Course I'll stick at it and see the back of this dump. But it'll be better when *you've* got yourself sorted and we can rent a room together down on the coast."

Chapter 12: June, 1964

The sun's rays scorch the pavement, sandwiching them in heat. Matty's gait is more crooked than Doris's as she tries to clench her private parts while hurrying along. Her burden would be intensified if she had allowed Neville to hold her hand, as Aidan is holding Doris's.

When Matty last stepped out with a gentleman, she would have sooner piloted a plane to Australia than visited him, unchaperoned, at home. But times have changed, the restrictions of her youth blasted back to history by the war. Yet propriety never goes completely out of fashion. There is a boundary, but no one has shown Matty where it lies.

If only her mother would advise her. But she has kept her counsel since before Matty launched into her monologue. Has she decamped because of Matty's showing off or is she equally flummoxed by modern etiquette? Doris – who now has wrapped her arm around Aidan's waist – is more worldly, but what she has learnt from marriage might not apply to single men. Matty ought to warn her. But, between her woozy brain and brimming bladder, she cannot accommodate another conundrum.

"Not far now," says Neville. "Aid's pad is the other side of the park."

Neville's *not far* could seem *miles* for Matty's waterworks and Doris's gammy leg. She cannot think beyond the pleasure of releasing a stream of urine, whether into the bowl of Aidan's lavatory or slap in the middle of the street. She cannot think beyond a pressure so intense it burns.

After crossing the road at a junction, instead of continuing down the terrace with the others, Matty mumbles she can't wait and veers off towards the relative privacy of a back lane. Trotting, waddling, her bloomers wetter with every step, she reaches the shelter of lines of laundry and crouches below a coal-shed hatch. Although her underwear is soaked and her shoes are splashed, she could dance for sheer bliss.

Until, tidying her clothing as best she can, she hears footsteps approaching. Fortunately, it is Doris who appears from between a pair of candy-striped sheets.

"Good idea." Balancing against the brick wall, Doris pulls down her bloomers and squats.

Turning away, Matty ferrets up her sleeve for her hanky. Nothing: she must have dropped it when they ran for the bus. She cannot show up to a party in sodden underwear, however hesitant she feels about attending. She needs some means of drying her crotch. "Have you still got those serviettes?"

Doris passes her a paper napkin. Matty stuffs it into her drawers. "Doris," she says, "I'm not sure about this party."

"You drew the short straw with Neville," says Doris. "But Aidan's cute."

"But is he a gentleman?" Matty fumbles for the right words. "Does he have honourable intentions?"

Doris laughs. "I hope not."

"You're not considering relations?"

"Why not? It's years since I've had a decent shag. Don't get me wrong, you can get it in Ghyllside if you know the hiding spots, but these ageing bones would be happier in a bed. Yours too."

Matty feels as rickety as the serviette disintegrating between her legs. They should never have left the asylum. "I couldn't."

Doris shrugs. "Don't then."

"Don't?" Declining brings other complications. She cannot drink tea and make small talk while Doris and Aidan frolic in bed. She cannot abandon her friend to the custody of strangers, even if they are professional protectors. "Let's get the bus back to Ghyllside, Doris." Sun stabbing her eyes is giving her a headache. The adventure has overrun.

"You please yourself, but I'm going with Aidan. I'll probably stay the night."

"You can't. Sister will be furious."

"Sister can go to hell. I'm informal, Matty. So are you."

Doris is already edging away when Matty opens her purse. "Take this. If anything happens, you can get a taxicab." If Doris takes the pound note, Matty should still have enough coppers for the bus.

Doris buries the note in the inside pocket of her waistcoat. Then she gives Matty a hug. "You're the best friend I ever had, posh girl. When me and Aidan get married, you can be matron of honour."

Matty's vision is blurred when Doris unpegs a couple of cotton headscarves from the nearest washing line. The one she gives to Matty depicts a fox-hunting scene and the one she shoves up her knickers is patterned with doves.

Matty shambles bow-legged towards the bus station. What will she tell Clara? What will she tell Sister if Doris does not return? The afternoon has been wasted. It is too late to see the circus now.

But too early to admit defeat and zip back to Ghyllside. Matty continues past the yawning entrance to the bus station. She can enjoy the ambience at The Cloffocks without watching the show. She can thrill to the sound of lions roaring in their cages and chimps chattering as if gathered for tea. Perhaps she will spot trapeze artists limbering up in their sparkly leotards. Perhaps she will see clowns outside their caravans, painting their faces or lacing up their banana-shaped shoes.

Despite being cheered by the prospect, her feet drag on the pavement. From behind, she hears the rumble of a bus leaving the hangar. Ahead, a woman in shorts, as if for the beach, emerges from a tobacconist's eating ice cream. To her right, a yapping dog runs alongside a bicycle, its tail almost caught in the spokes.

Here to the left, a tinted window fronts a display of bobbins, buttons and bolts of cloth; knitting patterns and sewing patterns; rolls of ribbon and lace. Windsor's Haberdashery: without Doris, she has lost her excuse to walk by.

Henry must be over thirty now, his father retired. Even in her shabby state, he will be delighted to see her. Unless he has forgotten she exists.

If she had kept the pound note, she could have purchased something in the shop while assessing the atmosphere. Or would it be easier to go straight to the point? The more she dallies, the harder it will be. But this is a greater challenge than exiting Ghyllside, a feat she mastered solely through Doris's support.

Now you have my assistance, says her mother. *I promise to stay by your side.*

Before she can change her mind, Matty pushes through the door. She marches directly to the counter and informs the girl she has come to see Mr Windsor.

"Is he expecting you, madam?"

Matty hesitates, but not for long. "Indeed he is. Although he would be unaware I was arriving today." Naturally, her mother's encouragement is more powerful than Doris's. After all, her mother worked in this establishment before Henry was born. Confidence pumps through Matty's bloodstream. Her brother will have yearned for this reunion as desperately as she has.

"I'll see if he's available." The shop-girl begins to withdraw. "May I ask who it is?"

"His sister."

As she waits, Matty fingers the fabric: crisp cotton; plush velvet; smooth silk. She will have a new frock made in pillar-box red with white polka dots to wear when she dines with her brother at the Wimpy Bar. Then they will cross the road to catch a film at the Ritz.

"Mr Windsor will see you now," says the shop-girl, indicating the spiral staircase to the office on the mezzanine floor.

Matty slips the straps of her handbag into the crook of her elbow so that she can grasp both the curving banister and the solid central pole as she mounts the steps. The gaps between the triangular treads make her dizzy the higher she climbs, as do the holes within them that are part of the cast-iron design. Yet it is difficult to avoid looking down.

Emerging bit by bit into the small office – head, torso, legs then feet – she is surprised and disappointed her brother is not waiting with open arms. Instead, he crouches over a desk strewn with foolscap and receipts, facing the window to the shop floor, his back to the entrance where Matty now waits. Although eager to embrace him, she relishes the opportunity to watch him working, swelling with pride that her baby brother has reached adulthood and a responsible role. As if part of her feared he would not make it, this man, so solid now, so business-like in rolled-up shirt sleeves, with pepper-and-salt hair razored above his neck. Her eyes well with tears but, to her surprise, she laughs.

The manager of Windsor's Haberdashery spins around. Appraising his visitor from eyebrows to ankles, he does not smile. The replica of his father, Matty would recognise him anywhere but, she realises, he cannot identify his beloved sister in her.

"I've telephoned the hospital," he says. "They're sending a car."

Matty has to touch the wall to steady herself. "Don't you know me? It's Tilly."

"I could see who it was the minute you came through the door." He indicates the observation window, serving the same purpose as the one on Ward 24. "I thought you'd pitch up sooner or later. You took your time."

His father has poisoned him against her. "Henry, dearest heart ..."

He laughs, but it is not only laughter that creases his features. This Mr Windsor is old.

"Oh, you poor soul, you *are* far gone, aren't you?" he says. "No, haberdashery has had its day. Henry works in accounts at the town hall." He half rises from his seat. "Let me get one of the girls to make you a nice cup of tea while you wait for your transport."

"You can't force me back there," says Matty. "I'm informal now."

"Perhaps you are, but you still need monitoring." He chuckles. "Look at the state of you. You had my assistant in a tizz. She came running up here, all in a flap. 'Mr Windsor,' she says, 'there's a *tramp* asking to see you.' Too polite to mention you stink."

Matty's cheeks are roasting as she stumbles down the stairs, almost tripping over her feet. She will not return to Ghyllside on *his* say-so. Not this time. She would rather bed the freckly fireman. "If I want tea, I shall go to the Wimpy Bar," she mutters, marching towards the door.

Outside, the urge to cry threatens her resolve. They have robbed her of her dignity. Squandered her youth. How tempting it feels to stop struggling, admit defeat and let them deliver her back to the hospital. She has no place in the modern world.

Hold up your head, my darling, says her mother. *You are a person, not a parcel. You can arrive under your own steam.*

She assumes her mother means her to take the bus rather than *walk* there. Matty dabs her eyes with her cardigan sleeve. As she does so, she realises she has not only lost her handkerchief, she has lost her purse, with all her money. Not lost, exactly, but left in her bag in the mezzanine office. She would rather crawl to Ghyllside than re-ascend that staircase.

You have not lost your brother, says her mother. Of course, she will seek him at the town hall. Working in accounts, his father said. A public servant, a superior profession to trading in cloth and thread.

Freshly inspired, Matty sets off, passing the bus station once more. Her route is in the same direction as Aidan's house. If she has no luck with Henry, then she will knock on doors until she finds her friend.

The traffic on the main road seems busier than previously. Matty waits at the kerb for a break in the flow so she can cross. A coal wagon passes and then – joy oh joy! – there is Doris dashing along the opposite pavement. Matty calls out her name.

Dearie me, if the shop-girl thought Matty dishevelled, she should be thankful she did not see Doris. Her flowery tea-dress is in tatters and a streak of mud or dried blood stains her neck. Matty can meet her brother another day. If Doris still has the pound note in her possession, they can ride to Ghyllside in the luxury of a taxi.

Although Matty can see her clearly, Doris appears not to notice Matty waiting at the kerb. She calls again and waves theatrically. The relief etched on Doris's face banishes Matty's humiliation. For a brief moment, they are the only two in the world.

Doris steps off the pavement. Matty hears an extended blast of a horn. The noise does not cease for minutes, hours, although the note varies: the lorry, the car, the ambulance siren. Her scream.

Chapter 13: June, 1940

My darling Henry,

What can I tell you when the truth is so unpleasant and I am weary of lies? What is the point of weaving stories I am forbidden to write? I will always remember you but perhaps it is better you forget you ever had a sister.

Until we meet again with our mother in heaven,

Tilly.

"Postlethwaite!"

Matilda was unaware she had been asleep until the nurse's screech juddered her awake. She wiped a thread of drool from her chin.

"Postlethwaite! Get your skates on, the doctor's ready for you."

A wraith lumbered from her seat in the corner of the dayroom, an expectant grin exposing a rack of blackened teeth. Shoulders hunched, she slunk towards the nurses' station. With a scowl, and arm extended, the nurse pointed her the opposite way.

Postlethwaite? If patients were being summoned alphabetically, Matilda should have preceded her in the queue. Unless Ghyllside ordered the letters differently or Matilda had forgotten a lesson learnt before she started school. "Nurse!" Matilda hurried to catch her before she closed the office door.

"What is it now, Osborne?"

Matilda drew courage from the use of her surname, although not enough to look the woman in the eye. She dropped her gaze to the fob watch pinned to the bib of her starched white apron. "Shouldn't I be next?"

A red needle marked ten seconds before the nurse deigned to reply. "What are you on about?"

"Seeing the doctor. I've missed my turn." Would the nurse take umbrage if Matilda alluded to the alphabetical confusion?

Instead, she laughed. "*You're* not on his list."

"Oh." Matilda's gaze dipped to the silvery latticework buckle on the nurse's wide elasticated belt. "I thought … I thought they were seeing everyone."

"You're mad keen to leave us, are you?"

Even staring at the nurse's black lace-ups, Matilda tried to stand proud. "I should like to do my bit for the war effort."

"You should like to, should you?"

Matilda cringed as the nurse aped her accent. Although it was disloyal to her mother, she cursed her childhood elocution classes.

"I'll ask if he can spare you five minutes when he's done with the others."

"You will?" Matilda felt as if she had grown a couple of inches as she dared to lift her gaze. When she smiled, the nurse brought to mind Sister Bernadette. But would she be like the nun who treated the fallen women at the convent with compassion, or like her alter ego who delivered Matilda to the asylum when she had thought she was going home?

"No harm in asking." Having dispensed her bounty, the nurse edged away. "But don't get your hopes up. He might say no."

Matilda would have liked to bathe and shampoo her hair, but she could not petition the nurse for another favour. She would have liked pen and paper to jot down her thoughts and clarify what she should say. She knew she must hide her intention to connect with her brother, but would her friendship with Doris help or hinder her case?

Doris had been gone for over a month. Discharged to a hostel attached to the munitions factory, and no word from her since. Doris squirmed when Matilda pushed her to promise to write as if, once lodged among normal people, she would absorb their prejudices against mental patients. Matilda felt hurt until the voice of her mother came through, asking whether Doris could read and write. Then she felt ashamed.

Matilda missed her. She missed her especially now, as she waited alone. Doris would stop her stomach churning with anticipation. Doris would dry her sweaty palms.

Time ticked by and no one called her. Nor did they call anyone else. The woman named Postlethwaite returned to the dayroom and curled up on a chair in the corner. Matilda could not bring herself to venture across and ask how her interview had gone.

When the nurse emerged from the office to line them up to march to the refectory for supper, Matilda assumed the doctor would have already left the hospital for his. But when she asked, the nurse said he was still on duty. She felt heartened when, claiming to have no appetite, the nurse gave her permission to remain on the ward.

The other patients returned from the refectory and settled into their chairs to snooze, stare into space or bicker with imaginary enemies until bedtime. Matilda sank lower in her seat. She had been forgotten or worse: remembered but deemed unworthy of the doctor's attention. But there was a chance, albeit a slim one, that the doctor had prolonged his shift into the evening to complete the assessments. Matilda resolved to wait. She had little else to do.

The patch of sky revealed through the window was daylight blue, but midsummer sky was deceptive: the sun did not set until ten. The doctor would not work *so* late. Besides, Matilda would be banished to bed by then.

She needed the lavatory: the pressure on her bladder made her wriggle in her seat. But she feared that the moment she left the room the doctor would send for her. She could not jeopardise her future by delaying a busy man.

The doctor smelled of mothballs and his hair was white. As were his shaggy eyebrows. A tag of loose skin hung from an upper eyelid. Matilda guessed that he and his suit had been recently revived from retirement to substitute for a younger man required for war. He beamed as he gestured her to the chair across the desk. "Good evening, Miss Osborne. What can I do for you?"

"Good evening, doctor." Having primed herself for more focused questions, Matilda was stumped. *What can I do for you?* Would *You can give me my discharge* be too direct? She would have to say something or he would dismiss her as an imbecile. "I wish to leave Ghyllside and contribute to the war effort."

"A noble sentiment." Leaning forward, the doctor put his elbows on the desk and rested his chin on his hands. "I can see you're on the road to reform."

"Thank you, sir." Matilda relaxed her shoulders but, not having risked a visit to the lavatory, she kept her thighs and buttocks clenched. "I've tried my best, I've worked hard and I've said my prayers, and I do understand I mustn't approach my brother in any manner, and I'll go wherever I can be most useful although, if at all possible, and if they still have vacancies, it would be lovely if I could be placed alongside Doris Fletcher at the munitions factory at Drigg." Reading his strained expression, Matilda reined herself in. "Of course, I'll do whatever you consider most suitable."

The doctor folded his arms. "I'm afraid you've lost me."

The gentleman is old enough to be your grandfather. You need to slow down.

Matilda glanced to where her mother's voice seemed to come from but, naturally, she could not *see* her idling by the glass-fronted bookcase. But she appreciated hearing her at least. "I do apologise," she told the doctor. "I'm simply so excited at the prospect of getting out." The doctor, she noted, appeared forlorn. "It's not that there's anything wrong with Ghyllside, but I shouldn't *be* here. I'm twenty years old. I want to get on with my life."

"Twenty-one."

"I beg your pardon, sir?"

"I was informed today is your birthday. You're twenty-one."

Matilda gasped. Her eyes watered and yet she laughed. How could she have forgotten? How could she have reached such a milestone with nothing to mark it? Without friends or family singing "Happy Birthday". With neither a card nor the tiniest cake.

"So I'm of age? I can discharge myself?"

"Regretfully, Miss Osborne, you may not leave until a psychiatrist decides you're fit."

"Haven't you done that? Didn't you say I'd reformed?"

"This isn't an official assessment, Miss Osborne. I merely meant to offer encouragement."

Matilda sensed her mother trying to get through to her, but a ringing in her ears blocked her message. "If it isn't an official assessment, why did you want to see me?"

"Nurse said *you*'d asked to see *me*. And, it being your birthday, we agreed you might be indulged."

"I wanted a discharge interview." Matilda wiped her eyes with the back of her hand. "Could we not do that now?"

"That isn't within my jurisdiction."

"Please!"

"Miss Osborne, control yourself!"

"I'm begging you." She felt her face contort with sobs.

"Discharge is solely at the discretion of the medical superintendent."

"Then tell him, please tell him, I'm ready to go."

"I thought I explained that this meeting is informal. But if I *were* to report on your condition, I could not discount what I have observed. Babbling. Emotional lability. Listening to voices."

As with the pregnancy, her misfortune boomeranged back to condemn her. If she acted strangely, it was due to injustice, not her character. But the authorities would never admit the fault lay with them.

Dampness in her bloomers compounded her humiliation. She tensed her muscles but could not stem the flow. The wet warmth spread from her buttocks to her stockings; soon it would pool on the parquet floor. The elderly doctor would add indecency to his list of her symptoms. Proof she was insane.

She thought of her mother and then of Doris as her hands formed fists. Her lip curled as she rose from her chair.

Matilda had tried to fend them off but they were too many. And too strong. Now, tightly bandaged in chill wet sheets, strapped to the bed in an otherwise deserted dormitory, she wondered how she would endure the next few hours until they came to unwrap her. If it had felt like torture with Doris beside her, how could she survive it alone?

If God were fair, He would punish the sinners. If God were generous, He would let her die. Yet, despite the restraints and the pressure on her chest, she continued to breathe. Inhaling stale air through her nose with the tang of disinfectant, releasing it through her mouth.

She had not struck the old gentleman. As soon as she saw his stricken expression, she pulled back. When the nurses arrived she was already repentant but, in their eyes, the damage was done. In her eyes also, albeit for different reasons. Certified insane, and with a propensity to violence, she would be trapped here for years. The war would be won without her.

"I thought you didn't like the wet packs."

Matilda gasped. Hearing her mother was natural; conjuring Doris was evidence she had lost her mind.

Rough fingers stroking her cheek. Could touch be an hallucination too?

"Aye, and a good thing I was already here on Disturbed."

"Is it really you?"

"Who else was you expecting?"

Matilda turned her head. It certainly looked like Doris crouching by the bed. Matilda began to cry.

"They're saying you skelped one of the doctors. Not even *I've* reached *those* heights of depravity."

"What are you doing here, Doris? Why aren't you at work?"

Dusting her knuckles, Doris grinned. "It doesn't match your standard of brawling, but I brayed my supervisor."

"At the factory? You hit her? How could you?"

"She was getting on my wick. Kept calling me loony. Wouldn't use my name."

"And they sent you back to Ghyllside?"

"Aye, and good job too. You've gone to rack and ruin without me."

It was selfish. Unchristian. But Matilda was glad Doris's foray into normality had been curtailed.

Chapter 14: July/August, 1964

"You've got to stop crying, Matty! It's making you ill."

Matty touches her cheek. The dampness could be from tears or from the lack of a clean towel in the bathroom when she last washed her face. How can she judge with her senses possessed by the pounding in her skull?

"I promise you'll feel better after a cuppa." From the blurred ranks of waiting-room chairs, a squat cup and saucer appears.

Matty knows she should take it, but her hands, exhausted by their recent explorations, are locked in her lap. Besides, the crockery is the colour of pus.

The fat rim of the teacup taps her lips. Top and bottom peel apart and lukewarm liquid trickles onto her tongue. It tastes of the bitter herbs the Lord fed to the Israelites. With the instruction to swallow, it slides down her throat. The sequence repeats but, when the cup knocks a third time, Matty's mouth stays shut.

"Come on, Matty! I haven't got all day. I've told you, the doctor's told you, even Matron's told you, it wasn't your fault. You've got to focus on the future, stop dwelling on the past.

And if you won't drink, they'll send you to the sanatorium and put you on a drip. You wouldn't like that, would you?"

Liking is immaterial. Think how Christ suffered on the cross. Her mother's voice banishes her headache momentarily. Long enough to accept another sip of tea.

"Atta girl." A plate materialises with two triangles of golden cardboard. "Can you manage a bite of toast?"

Such complex athletics. Matty no sooner surmounts one challenge than another emerges. Do they not realise solids could choke a corpse? The toast scrapes her lip.

"Is your head paining you? That's how you know the electric treatment's working. If you eat something, I can let you have a couple of aspirin. But not on an empty stomach. It could give you an ulcer."

Matty is being reincarnated as a rodent: mouth first, as her teeth nibble the toasted crust. She should ask the maid if hamsters have memories loud enough to make them weep. Matty's memories have been silenced, but her eyes still leak.

Amnesia is another side effect, says her mother. *Temporary, except where it is permanent.*

Before she was an animal, before she was Matty, she was Matilda. But Matilda told lies. It comes through to her now that they gave her the electric treatment to cut the cord connecting her to Matilda, casting her off from the bad things she believes were done to her and the worse things she did. Psychiatric exorcism to shock depravity from her brain. Aware now of a hole in her belly, Matty bites. Chews. Swallows.

"A swig of tea to wash it down?"

The cup substitutes for the plate. The hamster drinks.

Now the maid's face has freckles. Now her frock is palest blue. Across the room, a television croons. Smoke curls from cigarettes. Tobacco taints the air. Madwomen pace and shout.

"Can I leave you to finish it?" The saucer in her hands. The plate upon her lap.

The maid heaving herself from the chair activates a tremor in Matty's toes. It spreads through her feet in her tartan slippers and up her stockinged legs. The maid has already turned her back when the cup rattles on the saucer and the cold sheets of toast bounce on the plate.

The treatment has failed: Matty has not been reborn as a mindless creature. She is a person, with Matilda's memories intact. A sinner with a thumping headache and a duty to make amends.

Her brown skirt and orange sweater affront her. Why is she dressed so brightly? She must obtain a funeral frock. As she stands, toast flies, tea sails and crockery smashes on the floor. She rips off her jersey. Unbuttons her skirt and lets it drop to loop her ankles.

The maid grabs Matty's forearm and shakes her. "Put your clothes back on and fetch a brush and dustpan to clean up your mess. There's no excuse for this malarkey."

Matty shivers in her nylon petticoat, waiting for the room to cease spinning. She expects no respite from the torment in her head. Nor in her heart or her brain or wherever love is located. She has murdered her only friend.

The shocks should have eradicated her memories but, time after time, they come flooding back. If she had not abandoned her. If she had not waved. If she had been kinder, Doris would still be alive.

Every session promises oblivion. Every reawakening deepens the wound.

She did not attend the funeral. The doctors declared her too unwell. Matty is a child in a woman's body. With no rights to decide for herself. The person who, hands on hips, now glares at her is a nurse, not a maid. Matty is the skivvy, the patient, the slave.

Matty sits in the dayroom, lost in the fug of cigarette smoke and the jangling percussion of thirty vagabond women. On a table at her elbow is a glass of pink milk. Not a real glass, as Matty cannot be trusted with such a vessel. Once, she dropped a mirror and used the jagged edge to coax blood from her arm. It is written in her notes, so it must be true, although Matty cannot recall having access to a mirror and if anyone were a cutter it would be Doris.

Forget Doris.

Matty is not to be trusted with anything fragile. Only last week, or the week before, she was careless with a plate and cup and saucer, spilt the tea and toast the nurse had kindly brought her when she surfaced from ECT. Naturally she had to clean it up, despite the timpani in her head, which was only the electric treatment doing its business. Stamping on her sorrow, compressing her regrets into the teeniest tiniest corner of her mind. Naturally she had to gather the wreckage, with a nurse watching to ensure she picked up every shard and splinter and did not misuse them on her flesh. Naturally she had to fetch a pail of soapy water and scrub the floor on hands and knees, not only where she had been sitting but in a circle five chairs' width at either side.

Forget humiliation.

In fact, this was not punishment, but treatment, scientifically proven to prevent her making the same mistake twice. As one nurse told another, it had a name – overcorrection – designed to extinguish inappropriate behaviour in pigeons, patients and dogs. Along with chemicals and electricity, this new-fangled behaviour therapy would cure the hopeless cases and revolutionise psychiatry.

Forget false dawns.

Notice the plastic beaker, designed to mimic glass. Albeit lighter and shabbier, it serves the same function. It holds the pink milk at Matty's elbow. The not-glass will not leak or splash or lose the liquid. The not-glass is the epitome of fortitude.

Although she knows it tastes of powder – not strawberry, raspberry or any other ruddy fruit – Matty's stomach craves the milk. Her mouth is steeped in seawater. Her throat is caked in sand. But her arm is lazy. It will not shift from her side. Unless her arm moves, her hand will not reach the not-glass, her fingers will not claw around it. She cannot slake her thirst.

There is no hurry, says her mother. *You have your whole life to drink.*

They say she is making a good recovery. In a few more weeks, she will be well enough to lay flowers on Doris's grave. A nurse has promised to take her. But, if she is not sick, why does she need an escort to cross the grounds to the chapel? Yet, if she cannot raise her arm to lift the not-glass to her lips, how will she find the strength to push through the revolving doors?

One step at a time, says her mother.

Thus galvanised, as if it is as simple as blinking, Matty extends her arm, grasps the beaker and brings it to her mouth. Glug, glug, glug: powder-pink milk pours into her throat. Down it goes, past her tonsils and into her stomach. When the not-glass returns to the table, only a fraction of pink remains.

There now.

Matty rests her head on the chairback and closes her eyes. She is making a grand recovery. Tears roll hot down her cheeks.

A pinprick of red on her sleeve resembles blood, but sanity declares it a rosebud. Her flannelette gown is patterned with baby flowers. If those spots were blood, how would she explain the flecks of green?

It could be a mixture, says her mother. *You might have punctured your skin on a thorn.*

Like in the fairy tale. The princess pricked her finger on a spindle and slept for a hundred years. Sleep is a gift when no man nor beast could penetrate the forest to set her free.

Light drips from the windows to shine on dust motes and tendrils of smoke. Matty sits in the dayroom in her nightwear because her two skirts – the brown tweed and the blue-green tartan kilt – have been sent to the sewing room to have the waistbands adjusted. The nurses complain that, despite the electric treatment, Matty's body has shrunk.

The new Sister is indignant. She does not want a skeleton on her ward. "If you don't eat, you'll get sent to the sick bay. They'll push a hose down your throat and force-feed you. Like the suffragettes."

Matty does not want to be exiled to the sick bay. She drinks as much pink milk as she can. But when faced with anything more substantial, she remembers Doris's grave.

She had been all set to visit. Granted, she had no flowers, but her hair was tidy and her clothes were clean. But when she and the nurse arrived at the top of the steps on the other side of the revolving door, a taxi was waiting. Both driver and nurse expected Matty to climb in.

Doris is not buried next to Ghyllside chapel. Doris is buried at St Mark's, miles away. Matty can no more easily return to town than she can repeat her school days. She can no more travel by taxi than she can fly.

Forget Doris. Forget humiliation. Forget grief.

Sound advice, but forgetting creates an abyss. Who knows what horrors will rush to fill it?

"High time you stopped moping, Matty Osborne." Sister Henderson speaks through plastered make-up. "You're not the only one who's lost someone. Think of them bairns orphaned in the Blitz."

Whereas you still have me, says her mother.

"Think of them cattle trucks taking Jews to the gas chambers. Think of the folk behind the Iron Curtain and tell me you've got it bad. Living in this beautiful building, when some don't have a roof over their heads. Gorgeous grounds to roam around in, when some don't even have a pot plant to their name. Three square meals without lifting a finger and waited on hand and foot."

Mistress of all you survey.

"Anyroad," continues Sister Henderson, "I want you washed and dressed and a smile on your face the minute your skirts come back from the sewing room. And, after tea, we're having a social. A variety show and you, madam, are going to stand on your feet and recite a poem."

When the maids begin to clear the debris of breakfast, most of the guests drift to the lounge. Matty drifts along with them. Although her responsibilities leave her little leisure for socialising, she tries to grace them with her company at that hour. Her calm presence sets the community on track for a restful day.

The guests gravitate to the housekeeper's station, an enclosed compartment built into the wall, with a window into the lounge. Matty joins them.

"Get to the back of the queue!" barks a grey-haired guest with baby-blue spectacles slanting on her podgy face. "Dunno why *you're* bothering anyroad."

Naturally, Matty does not need to queue, but most of the guests appreciate the gesture, even if they lack the manners or vocabulary to say so. She does not condescend to reply to the disgruntled lady, but steps aside to show she respects their ritual. Her mother has hinted that the current houseguests are Catholic.

From her new vantage point, Matty can see the housekeeper in her office, head and shoulders hunched over her desk,

presumably listing the maids' jobs for the day. Two of them
stand on the lounge side of the glass, one checking names on a
clipboard, the other with a tray containing assorted packets of
cigarettes, like a cinema usherette. One by one, the guests shuffle
forward to collect a single cigarette from the appropriate pack.
When the clipboard maid has ignited the cigarette with a flame
from a plastic lighter, they huff and puff towards the chairs.

Although her mother advises against smoking, to protect her
voice, Matty is tempted. Stars like Bette Davis and Betty Grable
often pose with a tobacco stick between their index and middle
fingers, sucking up glamour, blowing smoke rings through ruby
lips. Now Matty turns away as the tip of the last cigarette begins
to glow.

The maid calls her back. "Did you want something, Matty?"

You have everything you need, says her mother. Yet Matty's
slippers skate forward.

The usherette maid takes her tray into the office. When Matty
follows, the housekeeper looks up. "Are you after your jelly
babies? Away and give us a poem first."

Hovering in the doorway, Matty spots the sweet jar on top of
the filing cabinet. It belongs to her, as the cardboard packs of
tens and twenties belong to the guests, and this closet provides
the optimum conditions for storage. But her sweets were a gift
from the maids for her recent birthday and, unlike cigarettes, it
is safe to consume more than one at a time.

Even gifts not wrapped and tied with ribbon come with
strings attached. So Matty does not hesitate to launch into the
housekeeper's favourite poem. She pegs her gaze to the jar of
inch-high edible children as she narrates the tale of Matilda, who

upset her aunt so much with her dreadful lies she burned to death in a house fire.

When Matty reaches the finale, the clipboard maid counts a dozen jelly babies into a brown paper bag. Matty watches to confirm there are sufficient yellow ones. "Off you go, then," says the housekeeper, handing them across.

Leaving the office, Matty clasps the bag to her chest and exits the dayroom before any of the guests come begging. She passes the dining room where a maid is laying the tables for luncheon; her mother insists on such tasks being undertaken well in advance.

Matty departs the ladies' quarters and descends the stairs. She presses against the tiled wall as a choo-choo train of empty breakfast trolleys trundles past to the kitchen. Still clutching the twelve jellies in assorted colours, Matty follows the corridor in the opposite direction. Her anticipation builds as she turns left towards the main entrance. Will the weather outside be sunny or dismal? Will any new guests, staff or visitors breeze in?

Although not always possible, Matty strives to be there to welcome newcomers to Ghyllside. Whether hall boy or butler, housekeeper or scullery maid, Matty endeavours to greet them with a smile. She is courteous and polite to journalists, whether from *Vogue* or the local rag. However tiresome, they cannot curb their appetite for tittle-tattle about the landed gentry.

As to the guests, many are refugees blunted by savagery and war. Most are weary from their travels in crowded cattle trucks or on foot. They may be coarse in behaviour and appearance, but Matty could not call herself a Christian if she denied them food and shelter. Indeed, it is a privilege to serve.

The teak-panelled vestibule is empty, save for the switchboard operator in her cubbyhole. Matty settles her derriere on the seat opposite. One by one, she removes the jelly babies from the paper bag and lines them up along the wooden bench. They will constitute the reception committee should someone special emerge from the revolving door.

Matty has never lost hope. Somewhere far beyond the estate boundary, somebody holds her in their heart. This person, who cares for her almost as much as her mother does, will find her eventually. Matty wants to be ready to be found.

Of course you might not recognise them, warns her mother. *Saviours tend to come in disguise.*

The shush of the revolving door heralds a new arrival. As shoes trip to the telephonist's window, Matty swaps a red jelly baby with a green one to lead the procession. When the visitor starts talking, Matty sneaks a glimpse.

She gulps. Would a chambermaid carry a shoulder bag so hefty it tilts her sideways? Would a journalist wear such flamboyant pantaloons? Would a guest sport such a vibrant fur hat?

That is not a hat, says her mother. *Her hair is radiant pink.*

Spiffing! As the Bohemian approaches, Matty conceals her excitement by arranging the jelly babies. She bites off the head of an orange one as an example to the others of the consequences of failing to give a good impression.

Someone must break the silence, but the visitor seems too shy to speak. Matty should not need to introduce herself, but how can she reassure the new girl Ghyllside is a fountain of tolerance? Her strange attire and – as a swift glance now attests – swarthy skin will not attract adverse attention, so long as she abides by the rules.

As the girl sighs, it comes through to Matty what makes her so splendid. Matty must communicate this new insight without causing alarm. "Did you run away from the circus?" The harem pants, the hair and the hue of her skin could not add up to anything else.

Yet the circus girl seems nonplussed. *Never mind,* says Matty's mother. *You will have other opportunities to display your largesse.*

Thank you for reading

Thanks for reading *Stolen Summers*. I hope it lived up to your expectations.

In fact, I'd love to know what you thought of it. Reader feedback helps me improve as a writer.

Plus, if you post a review online, you can help other readers decide whether the book is for them.

Go here linktr.ee/stolensummers or scan the QR code for direct links to the popular review sites

Alternatively, you can email me at annegoodwinauthor@gmail.com

When you're ready, I'd also like to offer you **some free fiction in the form of an e-book of prize-winning short stories** and to tell you about **what Matilda did next**. But first let me thank those who helped me transform a vague idea for a story into the finished book.

Acknowledgements

Huge thanks to the readers, reviewers and book bloggers who warmed to my character Matilda when she first appeared in *Matilda Windsor Is Coming Home*. You gave me the confidence – I might even say permission – to delve deeper into her history and I hope I've done justice to the woman you've taken into your hearts.

Almost anything I read can feed into my writing, but two books in particular were crucial to my research. When I turned to *Black Poppies* by Stephen Bourne to help flesh out the character of Eustace, I was shocked to learn about the race riots in 1919. Since one of my themes is social justice, I couldn't resist mentioning the shabby treatment of Black servicemen after the Great War.

Although I knew a lot about the history of psychiatry already, I hadn't come across the wet pack treatment until I read Joanne Greenberg's semi-autobiographical novel, *I Never Promised You a Rose Garden*. I highly recommend this novel – and the film based on the story – for its portrayal of a journey into mental disturbance and out again.

I'm indebted to Emma Ward, Kate Lewin and Paul K Joyce for incisive feedback chapter by chapter when this was a work in progress and to Clare Goodwin for helpful comments on the finished draft. Sara-Jayne Slack was a wonderful editor once again, while Michelle Watson and Clare Stevens meticulously proofread the work. Of course, any remaining errors are my responsibility alone.

Free fiction and keeping in touch

If you enjoyed *Stolen Summers*, why not help yourself to a free e-book of short stories, *Somebody's Daughter*?

Somebody's Daughter

What does it mean to have a daughter?
How does it feel to be one?

A child carer would do anything
to support her fragile mother.
A woman resorts to extreme measures
to stop her baby's cries.
A man struggles to accept
his middle child's change of direction.
Another uses his daughter
to entice young women into his car.
A woman contemplates her relationship
with her father as she watches a stranger
withhold his attention from his child.

Mothers of daughters, fathers of daughters,
daughters from infancy to middle age.
Three award-winning short stories
plus a couple more.

**Prize-winning short stories from the Polari Prize shortlisted
author of Sugar and Snails.**

"I had to limit myself to reading one story a day, because there was so much in each one
to mull over and consider. The author has such an evocative way
of expressing her characters - in so few words, she creates their whole world.
Heartbreaking, poignant, thought-provoking."

Annalisa Crawford,
author of *Small Forgotten Moments*.

Go to bit.ly/daughtershorts or scan the QR code for your free copy. This will also subscribe you to my email newsletter, which is the best way to keep in touch and hear about events, offers and new releases.

What's next for Matilda?

We left Matty in 1989, living an alternative reality but reasonably content. Would you like to know what happens next?

My follow-up novel, *Matilda Windsor Is Coming Home* is set in the 1930s and 1989-91. It relates the events leading up to her hospital admission and the attempts to resettle her in the community fifty years later.

Read *Matilda Windsor Is Coming Home* to gain an insight into Matilda's bond with her mother and why she continues to rely on her advice. In addition, you'll meet the circus girl, the pink-haired social worker determined to undo the damage of the past. You'll also meet her brother Henry, still searching for the sister he hasn't seen since he was six. Towards the end, you'll also discover the paternity of her 'illegitimate' child.

Matilda Windsor Is Coming Home

**In the dying days of the old asylums,
three paths intersect.**

Henry was only a boy when he waved goodbye
to his glamorous grown-up sister;
approaching sixty, his life is still on hold
as he awaits her return.

As a high-society hostess renowned
for her recitals, Matty's burden
weighs heavily upon her,
but she bears it with fortitude and grace.

Janice, a young social worker, wants to
set the world to rights,but she needs
to tackle challenges closer to home.

**A brother and sister separated by decades of deceit.
Will truth prevail over bigotry,
or will the buried secret keep family apart?**

Go to linktr.ee/matildawindsor or scan the QR code to order
a copy from your favourite retailer.

Here's a sample of what readers say about *Matilda Windsor
Is Coming Home*:

"Matty is an endearing character,
and I did not want the book to end."

'This is a beautiful story filled with compassion, brutality,
and lovely touches of humour.
It's one of my favourite reads this year."

"A book of kindness, positivity and hope."

"I smiled, I laughed but also wanted to sob at the same time."

'The author... knows how to grab your attention and draw you into
what proves to be one hell of a compelling read."

"As much a story of human resilience as it is of human frailty."

"This book will have you breaking your heart one minute
and laughing out loud the next."

"I can't imagine anyone reading this book and not being moved
by the characters. They draw you in and won't let you go!"

Still unsure if it's for you? Learn more about the three main characters in these short extracts from the novel.

Janice arrives at Ghyllside

A white P against a blue background: Janice was almost level with the sign when she swung the wheel to the left and shunted into the lay-by. A horn blared as a livestock lorry loaded with lambs sped past. Janice swore, but only the Snoopy swinging from the rear-view mirror heard her.

Silencing the engine, she scuffled into the passenger seat and stomped out onto the verge. Fisting the air, she dropped her jaw and screamed.

Traffic roared by, indifferent. The slate hillside wore the frown that had served it for millennia. A small brown butterfly danced from daisy to dandelion, oblivious. Throat tingling, Janice clambered back into the driving seat, grabbing a water bottle from her bag in the passenger foot-well on the way.

By the dashboard clock she had less than an hour to get to her appointment. Or to find a phone box to tell David Pargeter she'd changed her mind. She could scoff scones spread with Cumberland rum butter in a twee teashop, fuel for the drive home. Or skip the scones and take a detour via Huddersfield and ask her dad to fix the car door.

Was it really over with Stuart? Could love perish between the first and second slice of toast? She'd imagined a cottage on a dirt track, a couple of Labradors to fill the gap before babies. On summer evenings they'd walk the dogs after work, up to the fells or down to the shore. (Janice oscillated between a coastal idyll and one inland.) Senseless pitching up in the middle of nowhere without him. She'd be better staying in Nottingham among familiar faces, and with a wider selection of post-qualification jobs.

The last year of snatched phone calls and hours on the M6 was bound to be stressful. Juggling essays, lectures and placements while Stuart grappled two hundred miles away with his first grown-up job. But it wasn't only geographical separation that strained the relationship. Feet in different counties, their politics had drifted continents apart.

Janice wriggled in her seat, peeling her cotton trousers from her thighs. It wasn't the weather making her sweat: officially summer, the sun was a mere phantom in the clouds.

Nevertheless, she'd have felt more fragrant if she'd followed Stuart's advice and worn a skirt.

But how dare he challenge her choices? *You're not my mother,* she'd said, although Janice's mother would never ridicule her for *dressing like a student.* Ten months of ironing a clean white shirt every morning had consolidated Stuart's conservatism. And to think she'd defended *him.* When he'd got the job at Sellafield, Sheena would have come to the booze-up in a T-shirt proclaiming *Pigs Can Fly, the Earth Is Flat and Nuclear Power Is Safe* if Janice hadn't caught her.

With a shrug, Janice secured her seatbelt and drove off. She would decide at the next roundabout whether to continue on to the interview or head south.

Leaving the car park, the clock tower confirmed she'd made it with five minutes to spare. Despite being home to several hundred people, and workplace for as many staff, there wasn't another soul in sight. An aura of subterfuge enveloped Ghyllside – of deadness – as if behind the majestic facade lurked a yawning sinkhole, as if the roses in the turning circle were made of wax. Mounting the stone steps, Janice imagined mingling with the hapless new arrivals in the hospital's heyday a century before. The ache of rejection. The fear of never seeing a friendly face again.

Janice pushed through the revolving door to traverse the tiled floor of the vestibule to a window in the teak-clad wall. In a room barely bigger than a broom cupboard, the receptionist plugged and unplugged cables on the switchboard. "You take a seat, Miss Lowry," she said, when Janice stated her business. "Mr Pargeter will be with you in a jiffy."

A stab of nervousness took Janice by surprise. After all, she'd only come out of politeness. Or apathy. She didn't *want* the bloody job now. But interview practice was gold dust whatever the circumstances. Glancing around, she couldn't spot any rival candidates. Unless the frail woman mumbling into a paper bag was also about to qualify as a social worker. Janice watched her pluck a jelly baby from the packet, bite off its head, and add its body to the tail of a procession snaking the bench.

Engrossed in the etiquette of a parallel universe, she seemed unaware of Janice, too self-absorbed to shimmy along for her to sit or deposit her bag. Yet the woman raised her gaze. "Did you run away from the circus?"

"Pardon me?" Janice would have been less shocked if the walls had addressed her. And, had she credited the patient with a voice stronger than a whisper, and the will to use it, she'd never have imagined her speaking like royalty.

The woman inspected a yellow jelly baby and stuffed it up her cardigan sleeve.

Could this be part of her assessment? Was the telephonist-cum-receptionist observing from her cubbyhole, scoring her for empathy, warmth and genuineness on a Xeroxed sheet? "The circus?"

She was still awaiting a response when a tall man emerged from a door opposite the entrance. Janice drank in his casual get-up – open-necked shirt, mud-coloured cords and Jesus sandals with socks – and sensed him appraising hers. But he didn't blink at her pink hair, T-shirt and harlequin harem pants. If all the patients were as wacky as this woman, and the staff similarly offbeat, working at Ghyllside might be fun, with or without a boyfriend to go home to at night.

Henry still hopes

A no man's land between the poles of summer and winter, Henry's birthday month brought no excuse for celebration. Nature, never his ally at the best of times, was especially villainous in October, when weather conspired with trees to make the pavements a combat zone. Fallen leaves, wrenched from the wood by the wind, were bashed by rain and hail to a slippery sludge, causing Henry to hobble. Returning from work in the fading light, canine filth lay in ambush, camouflaged by leaf mould. The hostilities weren't solely underfoot: misted glasses stole his sight and his trilby proved a poor deterrent to conkers bombing from horse-chestnuts.

From as far off as number 38, he could tell his garden gate had been left open. Not unlatched or ajar but pushed back to align with next door's fence. Any old Toto, Duke or Lassie could mooch in and relieve itself amid the shrubs. The spaniel from number 51 was a prime offender, although when Henry had managed to catch its owner, the chap had the temerity to accuse *him* of negligence on account of a few un-nuked weeds.

After settling the gate between the posts, Henry approached The Willows. At least autumn brought reprieve from Irene's nagging to repair the concrete path. Or to sand and gloss the front door.

Stepping over the threshold, he retrieved his post from the doormat: the solution to the riddle of the unclosed gate. Three brown business envelopes, the addresses typed, unlikely to harbour news of his sister. Yet Henry's hopes could make a banquet out of crumbs.

Henry shed his hat and coat in the hallway and made for the kitchen. Dumping the letters temporarily on the draining board, he'd snapped the heads off three matches before his hand was sufficiently steady to ignite the gas beneath the kettle.

The first letter was an anti-climax: *his* address, some neighbour's name. Henry was damned if he'd hammer on doors to convenience a postman too idle to secure a gate. Grabbing a biro from the drawer, he pulled down the kitchen cabinet's hinged shelf as a makeshift desk, scored two bold lines across the envelope and printed NOT KNOWN AT THIS ADDRESS in between. That dealt with, he ripped into the other two envelopes. Even as he winced at the typewritten *Dear Mr Windsor*, he had to scan to the bottom to ensure neither carried the signature he'd waited fifty years to see.

A missive from Somerset House confirmed, *further to your recent enquiry*, there was no record of a marriage or death attached to the name Tilly Windsor. The correspondence shuttling to and fro at roughly six-monthly intervals was akin to having a pen-pal; Henry envisioned a homely secretary in cats-eye spectacles who would fret if he left too long a gap. Scooping dried leaves from the caddy to the Brown Betty, he caught himself humming. Once he'd eaten, he'd rattle off a batch of queries to provincial papers. Henry fancied tackling the Scottish islands, and South Rhodesia if time allowed.

Henry couldn't fathom the other letter. Linda Quinn could have walked to his desk sooner than dictate a memo. He re-read it while the tea brewed.

He'd been stunned to be passed over on the previous head's retirement. Robbed of the position by an outsider, and a woman at that. But, fair's fair, apart from her reverence for computers – a source of banter between them – she'd done a decent job. Rumour had it she wouldn't stick at head of payroll, either hopping up a rung to head of personnel or sheering sideways for the same title with a bigger budget at County Hall. Linda was conscientious; she wouldn't move on without nominating a successor. If she wanted to gauge Henry's interest, she was wise to do so discreetly.

At fifty-seven, he had three years to make his mark before collecting his retirement clock. Despite the darkness gathering beyond his kitchen window, Henry's prospects gleamed. Good things come in threes: he'd gain his promotion; Irene would ditch her husband; Tilly would come home.

Were their father alive he'd reproach Henry for counting his chickens. Yet *he* also followed his faith, bowing to the Great Architect of the Universe, along with his fellow masons at the Lodge.

Henry chuckled as he identified the tune he'd been humming: *White Christmas* in October! If *one* of his three wishes were granted, The Willows would host its merriest Christmas since his mother's day. Since before the war. Before the Depression. Before Henry was born.

Matty leaves Ward 24

The cushion sighs, squashed by a body sinking into the seat
beside her. Matty scrunches her already-closed eyes. She does
not care for distractions when she has a recital to prepare.
And, never able to anticipate *when* she might be called on to
deliver her lines, her day spools out as one continuous rehearsal.
Matty's burden weighs heavily upon her, but she bears it with
grace.

A whiff of lavender, but this is not her mother. Matty has
been deceived before. The breath is too loud, too erratic. A
smoker's lungs. Matty tilts her head away. Unmoored from the
monologue, she is obliged to return, silently, to the start.

Hands folded in her lap, she conjures her mother behind
closed eyelids. Mouthing the words from alongside the
orchestra pit, her features contorted to magnify the shapes
of the vowels. Matty smiles inwardly, as confidence courses
through her bloodstream. Although she can reel off the words
as readily as her name, her mother's prompting spells the
difference between fourth place with nothing to show for it and
a silken rosette.

"Matty!"

It cannot be anything important: her stomach signals it is too
soon after luncheon for afternoon tea. Poetry pattering in her
brain, she clenches her lips as if forming knots in party balloons.

"Matty, they'll be here shortly!"

Swallowing her vexation, Matty opens her eyes. A maid has
a cardboard box in her arms and a small brown suitcase by her
feet. "Are you leaving us, dear?"

The maid laughs, baring her teeth, which are in tiptop condition, remarkably so given the lack of affordable dentistry for the lower ranks. "No, but you are. They'll be coming any minute from Tuke House."

"Tuke House?" Matty knows of the Palladium and the Royal Albert Hall. She knows of the Folies Bergère, despite its salacious reputation. She has never heard of Tuke House. "Thank you, dear, but the current arrangements are tickety-boo."

As the maid flashes her teeth again, Matty studies her maw for a wink of precious metal. The prince gave her mother a pair of gold molars to match her wedding band, but when Matty's were due for renewal she'd made do with plastic.

"We packed your things this morning, remember?" Dipping into the box, the maid parades the bric-a-brac piece by piece: a chunky book with a crucifix on the cover; a crumpled brown-paper bag of chewies; a conker; a poorly-composed photograph of a boy balancing the Eiffel Tower on his head. Is this one of her mother's parlour games?

"You're going up in the world, Matty Osborne." Intent on memorising the contents of the box, Matty failed to notice the housekeeper encroaching. "Seems you're too good for us now."

I am? The housekeeper is never uncertain. Never wrong. If *she* thinks Matty is leaving, it would be unwise to contradict her.

Fishing in her pocket, Matty produces a palmful of coins. "Will this do for the taxicab?"

"Save your coppers for jelly babies," says the housekeeper. "It's a five-minute hop to Tuke House. You know, the annexe where the sanatorium used to be?"

"We went for a visit yesterday," says the maid. "Found your bed in the dormitory and had a cuppa in the lounge."

The memory roasts her cheeks. The butler, whose coarse accent and casual apparel led her to mistake him for a hall boy or porter, addled her further by asking how she took her tea. As if there were any alternative to *the way it comes*! Yet beneath that unfortunate incident lies a pleasanter proposition, if she can locate it. Matty shuts her eyes.

When she opens them, the answer appears before her. "Good afternoon, Ms Osborne," says the circus girl. "May I escort you to your new abode?"

From her plume of pink hair to her patterned harem pants, the circus girl is as cheery as a rainbow scuttling a storm. How was this bohemian character recruited to a country house? Matty will shower her with honours to prevent Bertram Mills and his cronies luring her back to the Big Top. She springs to her feet.

"Hi there, Matty." Even here, in the ladies' quarters, the butler is informally attired, in a handyman's blue jeans and a school gym shirt. "Haven't you any outdoor shoes?"

Matty checks her feet, colourfully shod in tartan slippers with a red faux-fur trim. What need has *she* for outdoor shoes? The man must be a communist, bent on bamboozling her with his rhetoric.

"Shoes?" says the housekeeper. "She's not scaling Scafell Pike." Nevertheless, she urges Matty to resume her seat. Then, after directing the maid to open the suitcase, she kneels on the floor to exchange Matty's slippers for leather shoes the colour of the conker, albeit with less of a shine. Matty *must* have been promoted for the housekeeper to fasten her shoelaces like a shop-girl in Browne's.

Helping her to her feet, the housekeeper whispers a warning, "Don't get too comfy, mind. You'll be back in two shakes of a cuddy's tail."

Matty feels something stir below her breastbone as her gaze flits between the housekeeper and the circus girl. A snip of rebellion wizened with neglect. As the feeling blooms, it comes through to Matty that her mother would not appoint this person to the position of housekeeper. She has been duped by her imperial bearing and midnight-blue dress. She should have detected something foxy in the thickly pancaked makeup. One cannot trust a person who prepares her face for the stage but never deigns to recite.

Matty links arms with the circus girl. She is leaving for a more appreciative audience. No, she will not be coming back.

Order a copy from your favourite retailer via this link linktr.ee/matildawindsor or by scanning the QR code

About the Author

Anne Goodwin's drive to understand what makes people tick led to a career in clinical psychology. That same curiosity now powers her fiction.

Anne writes about the darkness that haunts her and is wary of artificial light. She makes stuff up to tell the truth about adversity, creating characters to care about and stories to make you think. She explores identity, mental health and social justice with compassion, humour and hope.

An award-winning short-story writer, she has published three novels and a short story collection with small independent press, Inspired Quill. Her debut novel, *Sugar and Snails*, was shortlisted for the 2016 Polari First Book Prize.

Away from her desk, Anne guides book-loving walkers through the Derbyshire landscape that inspired Charlotte Brontë's *Jane Eyre*.

Find her on her website annegoodwin.weebly.com

Also by Anne Goodwin

Novels

Sugar and Snails (Inspired Quill)
Underneath (Inspired Quill)
Matilda Windsor Is Coming Home (Inspired Quill)

Short story collections

Becoming Someone (Inspired Quill)
Somebody's Daughter (Annecdotal Press)

Lightning Source UK Ltd.
Milton Keynes UK
UKHW042251261022
411157UK00004B/356